William Does His Bit

Just—William
a facsimile of the first (1922) edition

The William Companion
by Mary Cadogan

Just William's World – a pictorial map
by Gillian Clements and Kenneth Waller

* A hardback edition of this title is available from
Firecrest Publishing Ltd, Bath, Avon

BEFORE EITHER OF THEM COULD STOP HIM, WILLIAM HAD
CAUGHT HOLD OF MR. BALHAM'S MOUSTACHE AND PULLED
IT AS HARD AS HE COULD! *(See page 17)*

William Does His Bit

RICHMAL CROMPTON

Illustrated by Thomas Henry

MACMILLAN CHILDREN'S BOOKS

First published 1941

First published in this edition 1988 by

MACMILLAN CHILDREN'S BOOKS
A division of Pan Macmillan Children's Books Limited
London and Basingstoke
Associated companies throughout the world

Reprinted 1990, 1991, 1992

British Library Cataloguing in Publication Data
Crompton, Richmal
  William does his bit.
  Rn: Richmal Crompton Lamburn   I. Title
  II. Henry, Thomas
  823′.912[J]   PZ7

ISBN 0–333–46673–X

Phototypeset by Wyvern Typesetting Ltd, Bristol
Printed in England by Clays Ltd, St Ives plc

Contents

An invitation from William

Join my club and becum a nOutlaw
William Brown

You can join the Outlaws Club!
You will receive
✳ a special Outlaws wallet containing
your own Outlaws badge
the Club Rules
and
a letter from William giving you the secret password

To join the Club send a letter with your name and address written in block capitals telling us you want to join the Outlaws, and a postal order for 45p, to

The Outlaws Club
Children's Marketing Department
18–21 Cavaye Place
London SW10 9PG

You must live in the United Kingdom or the Republic of Ireland in order to join.

Chapter 1

William Does His Bit

William was finding the war a little dull. Such possibilities as the black-out and other war conditions afforded had been explored to the full and were beginning to pall. He had dug for victory with such mistaken zeal—pulling up as weeds whole rows of young lettuces and cabbages—that he had been forbidden to touch spade, fork or hoe again. He had offered himself at a recruiting office in Hadley, and, though the recruiting sergeant had been jovial and friendly, and had even given him a genuine regimental button, he had refused to enrol him as a member of His Majesty's Forces.

"You're not quite big enough," he had said. "There's very strict regulations about size."

"I grow quick," pleaded William. "I'm always growin' out of things."

"Not quite quick enough for us," said the sergeant firmly.

"Well, can't I be a drummer boy?" said William. "I can make a jolly fine noise on a drum. An aunt of mine said it made her head ache for weeks. I bet it'd scare ole Hitler off all right."

"No vacancies for drummer boys at present," said the sergeant.

"Well, will you let me know when there are?" said William.

"Certainly," said the sergeant, but he winked at a corporal standing near as he spoke, and William didn't set much store by the promise.

He next wrote to the Premier to offer his services as a spy, but received no answer. Thinking that it had been intercepted by German agents, he wrote again but still received no answer. He decided that he could at any rate practise being a spy, so went out wearing Robert's hat and coat, but, despite the corked moustache that was supposed to conceal his identity, he was instantly recognised by Robert and his ears boxed so soundly that he reluctantly abandoned his spy career.

"Cares more about an ole coat an' hat than winnin' the war," he muttered indignantly. "He oughter be put in prison, carin' more for an ole coat an' hat than winnin' the war."

He had almost given up hope of being allowed to make any appreciable contribution to his country's cause when he heard his family discussing an individual called "Quisling" who apparently and in a most mysterious fashion existed simultaneously in at least a dozen places.

"I bet there's one of 'em in England," said Robert darkly. "Getting things ready or *thinking* he's getting things ready. . . . Gosh! I'd like to get my hands on him."

"But who *is* he?" said William.

"Shut *up*!" said Robert. "They're jolly well going to put a spoke in his wheel in Turkey. They never expected to find him in Holland or Belgium!"

"Holland or *Belgium*?" said William. "Thought you said he was in Holland or Turkey. Thought——"

"Shut *up*!" said Robert and went on darkly: "And he's right here in England, too. We'll have to keep our eyes open."

William was past further query or comment.

He tackled his mother, however, the first time he found her alone.

"I say," he said, "who is this Grisling man?"

"Quisling, dear," corrected his mother.

William waved the objection aside.

"Sounds the same." he said. "Anyway he *can't* be in Turkey *an'* Belgium *an'* Holland *an'* England at the same time. No one could. Robert's cracked, sayin' he can be."

"Well, dear, he's not really the same man." said Mrs. Brown. "He's a sort of—*type*."

"What's that?" demanded William. "Thought it was a kind of dog."

"No, dear," said Mrs. Brown patiently. "This particular man was a Norwegian and helped the Germans to get a footing in his country, and other people in other countries who try to do the same are all called Quisling."

"Why?" said William. "Why can't they call them by their real names?"

"They don't know what their real names are."

"Why don't they ask them?"

"Really, William," said Mrs. Brown helplessly, "I can't explain it any more. Go out of doors and play."

"Well, listen," pleaded William. "Tell me jus' one thing. How do they do it? How do they get people to let ole Hitler in?"

Mrs. Brown sighed resignedly.

"I'm not quite sure, dear. I think they sort of make people believe that they'd have no chance of resisting him and so it's best to let him in. They try to frighten people. At least, I think that's it."

"Why doesn't the gov'ment lock 'em up?"

"They don't know who they are."

"Thought they knew they were called Grisling."

"No, dear, they don't."

"I 'spose they *pretend* they're called other things jus' to put the gov'ment right off the scent."

"Yes, I suppose they do," said Mrs. Brown, settling down to darn a pile of table napkins.

"They might pretend to be called anythin'."

"Yes," agreed Mrs. Brown. "I suppose they might. This linen really ought to have worn better. If it weren't for the war I shouldn't trouble to mend them at all."

"There might be one here pretendin' to be called anythin'."

"I suppose so, dear. . . . It's partly the laundry, of course. They simply *maul* things."

"An' I bet no one knows who he is. If they did they'd have him in prison."

"What are you talking about, dear?" said Mrs. Brown, bringing her mind with an effort from the composition of a projected letter of complaint to the laundry.

"Ole Grissel," said William.

"Grissel? Oh, I know what you mean. He isn't called that, but I've forgotten just for the moment what he is called."

"Bet I'd catch him all right if I was the gov'ment."

"He's not alone, of course, dear. He has a lot of people working under him. It's a very complicated organisation, I believe. . . . Now, William, do leave that table napkin alone. It was just a weak place before you started pushing your fingers through it, and now it's a real hole."

"Well, I'm sorry," said William. "I didn't know it was goin' to go through like that. I hardly pushed at all. . . . Well—look here, are they *tryin'* to catch this ole Grissel?"

"I expect so, dear."

"I bet they're not," said William darkly. "I jolly well

bet they're not. Why didn't they catch him in Norfolk, then?"

"It was Norway, dear, not Norfolk."

"Well, why didn't they? I don't b'lieve they're tryin' at all. An' he's goin' about same as you or me. It might be anyone. It might be someone we know. It might be Robert, 'cept that he's not got enough brains for it."

"Well, William, you can't do anything, so stop worrying about it."

"*Can't* I?" said William. "*Can't* I do anythin'? You jus' see if I can do anythin'. I bet I can."

He walked out of the house and down the village street, scowling darkly.

Couldn't he do anything! He'd caught one German spy at the beginning of the war (more by good luck than good management, as even he had to admit), and didn't see why he shouldn't catch another. This was a different sort of spy, but if the government wasn't catching ole Grissel—well, there was nothing for it but to have a shot himself. Perhaps he was here—*here* in the village or in Hadley or in Marleigh. He'd got to be going round scaring people somewhere all the time, so he might as well be here as anywhere else. His face took on that expression of ferocity that betokened firm resolution. The more he thought about the matter the more convinced he was that old Grissel was somewhere in the neighbourhood. William, in whom the zest of the chase was up-rising fiercely, decided that there was not the slightest doubt that he was here. And if he was here, he'd got to be caught, and, if he'd got to be caught, then William was going to catch him. He realised that he must go very carefully. He had a master criminal to deal with and one who would stick at nothing. But there was not a moment to be lost. He must start at once.

He started by a tour of the village. Much to his

disappointment, an exhaustive search revealed nothing suspicious. He was at first tempted to suspect the vicar or the doctor of being ole Grissel in disguise, but after a few moments' reflection, he came reluctantly to the conclusion that their normal routine would leave them little or no time for criminal activities. The doctor, in particular, he was unwilling to cross off his list of suspects. The last draught the doctor had compounded for him, on his pleading that he felt too ill to go to school, had been so nauseous that William considered he had narrowly escaped death by poison.

He turned his steps from the village towards Hadley. There, though he followed several false scents, and annoyed several houscholders by staring in at their windows, he was no more successful. He retraced his steps to the village and made his way to Marleigh, where he couldn't even find any false scents. Dejectedly and having by now almost but, being William, not quite, given up hope, he went on towards Upper Marleigh.

The main road seemed to be empty except for two women who were approaching each other from opposite directions. William looked at them without interest. He wasn't interested in women at the best of times, and just now he wasn't interested in anything at all except ole Grissel. But, as he passed them, he heard something that made him stop and listen attentively.

"What's the codeword to-day?" he heard one of them ask.

He couldn't hear the answer, but the question was enough. A codeword. Spies. . . . Members of ole Grissel's gang. . . . They looked just two ordinary women—the sort that went to Mothers' Meetings and Women's Institutes—and all the time they were members of ole Grissel's gang. It had been careless of him not to have realised that they might be. Naturally ole

Grissel's gang would disguise themselves as people like that to put the government off the scent. Well, he'd found them now and he must shadow them till he ran ole Grissel himself to earth. He studied the two conspirators with interest. One was carrying a shopping basket and the other a string bag full of vegetables, but they'd probably got revolvers and things hidden among the cabbages and groceries and wouldn't scruple to use them. He drew nearer and, stooping down, pretended to be doing up his shoe lace.

"Aren't greens a price?" one of them was saying and the other replied:

"Yes, aren't they! And there don't seem to be half the lettuces about this year. Ours were no good at all—I can't think why."

They'd seen him, of course, thought William, and were talking like that to put him off the scent. Or—more probably—they were talking in code. Perhaps "Aren't greens a price?" meant "Let's kill Churchill", and "There don't seem to be so many lettuces about this year" meant "Heil Hitler"—or something like that.

They were separating now—each going on her way. For a moment William stood irresolute, wondering which to follow. One was going towards the village, the other—the one who had asked what the codeword was—was turning down a side lane off the main road. He decided to follow the second one. . . .

She went down the lane and in at the gate of a large building that William knew to be a school. It was the summer holiday and the building was empty. She went round to the side and in at a small door. It must be the headquarters of ole Grissel's gang. A jolly good idea, choosing an empty school in holiday time down a side lane like this. He decided not to follow her into the building. Peaceful and deserted though it looked, it probably bristled with concealed machine-guns and snipers and booby traps. Instead, he would inspect the building as best he could from the cover of a belt of variegated laurel that surrounded it. He dived into the nearest bush just in time, for two other women had just arrived and were going in by the same door as the first. They, too, looked the Mothers' Meeting—Women's Institute type. Evidently that was the particular disguise adopted by this particular band of conspirators. . . .

William made his way round one side of the building, still under cover of the laurels. It was disappointing in that it contained no window. Nothing daunted, however, he started on the second side. And there he was rewarded, for he suddenly came upon a screen of sandbags and, creeping round the screen, found a

CAUTIOUSLY WILLIAM HOISTED HIMSELF ON TO THE WINDOW-SILL AND PEEPED IN.

window, covered with black paint but conveniently open at the top. Cautiously he hoisted himself on to the window-sill and peeped in. He saw a cellar-like room, roughly furnished with a long trestle table and some chairs. The women he had seen entering had removed their hats and were taking their places at the trestle table. Others were putting on their hats and preparing to depart. William's eyes roved round the room. A man, who was evidently in charge of proceedings, sat at a small desk covered with papers. Ole Grissel . . . ole Grissel himself! He didn't look as William had imagined ole Grissel would look—he was undersized and stooping and had a small worried moustache—but he was

A MAN, WHO WAS EVIDENTLY IN CHARGE OF PROCEEDINGS, SAT AT A SMALL DESK COVERED WITH PAPERS.

obviously in charge and so he must be ole Grissel. On a table just beneath the window a large map was outspread. By craning his neck William could see that it was a map of the district. He could see Marleigh and Upper Marleigh marked on it quite plainly. There were little flags jotted about. Gosh! They had everything ready for ole Hitler! He could even see the road marked where his own home was. Going to hand over his own home to ole Hitler, were they, he thought, indignantly— with Jumble and his pet mice and his collection of caterpillars and his new cricket bat. The idea of this infuriated him more than any of the previous German outrages. He set his lips grimly. Well, if Hitler thought he was going to get his pet mice and his new cricket bat, he was jolly well mistaken. He realised that two of the women sitting at the trestle table were telephoning. He listened in amazement.

"Wrecked aeroplane causing obstruction in Marleigh Road. . . . Fire raging in Pithurst Lane. . . . Houses in Hill Road collapsed. . . . Marleigh police station blown up. . . ."

His eyes and mouth opened wider and wider. There wasn't a word of truth in it from beginning to end. He'd walked along Marleigh Road less than five minutes ago. . . . He'd passed Marleigh police station—and even exchanged badinage with a stout constable who was sunning himself in the doorway. The school building was in Pithurst Lane, and Hill Road was at the end of it. And all lay peaceful and intact in the summer sunshine, while this gang of Grissel confederates were broadcasting these outrageous lies. Propaganda. That was what it was, of course. Broadcasting lies right and left! Same as old Gobbles. One of the women was moving little flags about on the map.

"I haven't any more incendiary bomb flags, Mr.

Balham," she said to the man at the desk.

(William made a mental note of the name ole Grissel was calling himself.)

The man opened his desk and gave her a little box, and William, to his intense indignation, saw her put one on the road where his own home was. Huh! Ole Hitler was probably thinkin' he'd get his cricket bat by the end of the summer. *Huh!* The women at the telephones read out their pieces of propaganda (the latest was "electric light main, coal gas main and water mains all damaged. No repair parties available. Gas escaping. Fires in vicinity beyond control") from sheets of paper and, when they had finished, they handed them to the man at the desk, who put them on to a file. William could have watched this absorbing performance all morning, but an incautious movement made him lose his foothold. He fell down heavily and by no means soundlessly to the ground. After that he deemed it advisable to retire to his screen of laurel. At first he was afraid that the conspirators might send out an emissary to investigate and exact vengeance, but, to his relief, no one came.

He sat in the shelter of a particularly luxuriant laurel and considered his next step. He had discovered the nest of traitors, of course, but that wasn't enough. He must bring them to justice. And he knew that this wasn't as easy as it sounded. He hadn't read crime fiction for nothing. He realised that criminals whose meeting-place is discovered simply vanish from it, leaving no trace, and meet somewhere else. No, he must run the arch-traitor to earth—find out where he lived and all about him—before he attempted to bring him to justice.

He had waited, as it seemed to him, several hours when at last the small, insignificant-looking figure of Mr. Balham appeared, coming round the side of the building towards the main gate. William, from his hiding-place, studied his quarry with interest. The drooping moustache was, of course, a disguise. So were the spectacles. The stoop was probably a disguise, too. If he stretched right up he'd be quite a tall man. Well, nearly quite a tall man. . . . But he was disappearing down Pithurst Lane now, and William, turning up the collar of his jacket, drawing his cap down over his eyes in the conventional fashion of the sleuth, prepared to follow him. Had Mr. Balham chanced to turn round, he would have been much surprised by the antics of the small boy behind him, who dived into the ditch, scrambled along under cover of the hedge, hid behind trees for no apparent reason, and occasionally stopped to place twigs in a complicated pattern by the roadside. (These last were intended as signs to lead future investigators to the scene of the crime if the criminal suddenly whipped round and kidnapped or murdered him.)

Happily unaware that he was being shadowed in this sensational fashion, Mr. Balham turned into Hill Road (which he and his fellow conspirators had so recently reported bombed) and, opening the garden gate of a small, neat, newly built villa, disappeared inside a small, neat, newly painted front door. William stood in the road and stared at it, slightly nonplussed. He'd found out where the traitor lived, and so the moment seemed ripe for bringing him to justice, but he realised that even now the enemy might elude him. He had, in fact, come out into the garden in his shirt sleeves and was pushing a microscopic mowing machine round the microscopic front lawn. It was, of course, all part of the disguise. He was pretending to be an ordinary man, mowing an ordinary lawn, and (he had just stopped to do it) picking ordinary green flies off ordinary rose trees. If he told the police that this man was Grissel, the arch-traitor, they would just laugh at him. No, he must find some actual proof. His eyes wandered over the neat, respectable-looking little house. It was probably full of proof if only he could find it—letters and telegrams in code and confidential documents. Traitors always had confidential documents which they burnt when they saw the police coming. So that, even if William managed to persuade the police to come, the man would see them coming and at once burn all his letters and telegrams and confidential documents. Somehow or other William must get hold of the confidential documents himself. . . .

It would be jolly dangerous, of course. Ole Grissel would stick at nothing if he found him looking for them. In most of the crime stories William had read the hero was caught by the villain, but the police arrived in the nick of time. He must arrange for the police to arrive in the nick of time. . . .

* * *

Mr. Balham, A.R.P. Communications Worker, Supervisor of Marleigh Report Centre, put on his slippers and sank down into his favourite armchair with a sigh of relief. He had had a tiring day. First of all there had been the air-raid exercise down at the report centre, and he always found those rather exhausting. Then he had put in two hours' gardening, and he always found that extremely exhausting. He was glad to relax and to lose himself in his detective novel. The hero of the novel was alone in his flat when there came a ring at the door. He went to open it and found a policeman there.

"Sorry to disturb you, sir," said the policeman, "but we've just received a message asking us to come round here."

At that moment Mr. Balham's own door-bell rang, and he put the book aside with a little "Tut, tut" of exasperation. Some interruption always seemed to come at the most exciting point of a story. On his way to the door, he thought idly how strange it would be if he found a policeman there saying: "Excuse me, sir, but——"

He stopped on his way through the hall to straighten a mat, then opened the front door, assuming the forbidding expression of one who wants to get back to his detective novel as quickly as possible.

A policeman stood there.

"Excuse me, sir," he said, "but——"

Mr. Balham was so much astounded that he didn't hear the end of the sentence and had to ask the policeman to repeat it.

"We've had a message asking us to come round here."

The hall whirled round Mr. Balham for a moment, but with an effort he caught hold of it and put it right way up.

"I beg your pardon," he said, wondering if he had dropped off over the book and this were one of those fantastic dreams he had occasionally.

"We had a message to come round here," repeated the police.

"I never sent any such message," said Mr. Balham, looking down at his legs in sudden apprehension and being reassured by the sight of his neat and decent grey flannel trousers. The oddest things happened to him in his dreams sometimes!

"Well, it was certainly a queer sort of message," the policeman was saying. "Wouldn't give no name and sounded to me like a disguised voice. Told us to send round here in half an hour's time. Practical joker, probably—you'd be surprised the number we get—but it was on my beat so I said I'd look in."

"Well, I certainly never sent for you," said Mr. Balham firmly, "so it must be a practical joke."

"Probably," said the policeman, "but now I'm here I

might as well have a look round."

Entering the house he began a tour of inspection, followed by Mr. Balham, who had now come to the conclusion that this was no dream, but a Coincidence, such as people wrote to the papers about and recounted in clubs. He was wishing that he'd finished the chapter before the police came. It would be interesting to know what the police discovered in the hero's flat.

Well, certainly there was nothing to discover here. . . . But he was mistaken. There was something to discover. For at that moment the policeman threw open the dining-room door and discovered a small boy kneeling in front of the open sideboard cupboard, surrounded by silver teapot, jug, sugar basin, spoons, knives and forks and dishes—by a choice little collection of old silver, in fact, that Mr. Balham had recently inherited from a great-aunt.

After ringing up the police and arranging, as he thought, for them to rescue him from the hands of the villain in the nick of time, William had set out for Mr. Balham's house. There, he had effected an entry by means of a drain-pipe and an open bedroom window, and had begun a systematic search for the confidential documents. A thorough examination of Mr. Balham's bedroom had revealed nothing (though on visiting it later in the evening that mild man was to use language that would almost certainly have induced his great-aunt to alter her will), and so William had crept cautiously and silently downstairs and started on the dining-room. The sideboard cupboard had seemed a likely hiding-place and, finding it full of silver, William had taken it out piece by piece in order to make sure that the confidential documents were not hidden among them. It was at this moment that Mr. Balham and the policeman entered. They stood and stared at him in silence. Then

IT WAS AT THIS MOMENT THAT MR. BALHAM AND THE
POLICEMAN ENTERED

the policeman said to Mr. Balham:

"That your boy?"

"No," said the amazed Mr. Balham. "Never seen him before."

William looked sternly at the policeman.

"You've come a bit too soon," he said.

The policeman looked down at him.

"Yes," he said drily, "I can see I have."

"I've not found anythin' yct," said William.

The policeman looked down at the silver.

"You don't seem to have done so badly," he said.

"The only things of value in the house," said Mr. Balham.

"Oh, yes, he knew what to come for, all right," said the policeman. "A proper haul he'd got, too. Or would have had if I hadn't come along. . . . I don't know who you're working with, my lad, but whoever it is has given you away. We had a telephone call asking us to come along and nab you."

"*Me?*" said William in amazement. "It wasn't to nab me—it was to nab *him*." He pointed to Mr. Balham who was gazing down at him sadly. "*He's* the one you've gotter nab."

"That's a good one!" chuckled the policeman.

"Juvenile crime!" said Mr. Balham, shaking his head mournfully. "I've heard a lot about it, but I little thought to have it brought home to me like this. Why, he's a mere child!"

"Lucky for us we got that call," said the policeman. "Ten to one he'd have got away with it if we hadn't. Yes, young feller-me-lad, if someone hadn't rung us up and told us to come along here——"

"It was *me* rang you up," said William. "I tell you, it's *him* you've gotter get hold of. He's the crim'nal, not me. Look!"

Before either of them could stop him, he had caught hold of Mr. Balham's moustache and pulled it as hard as he could.

Mr. Balham gave a yell of anguish.

"Assault!" he said, nursing his face tenderly in both hands. "Add assault to your charge, constable. Theft and assault. And I hope the magistrate won't be lenient."

"He's got it stuck on jolly fast," said William, "or else

he's grown it. I bet that's it. He's grown it. . . . But it's a disguise, all right."

The policeman took out his notebook.

"I want your name and address, my lad," he said, "and an explanation of what you're doing with that silver."

"*Me?*" said William indignantly. "Look here! You don't understand. It's not me what's the criminal. It's *him*. He's ole Grissel. He's handin' the country over to ole Hitler. I tell you, I've *seen* him doin' it. He was doin' it all this mornin'. *Listen*. If you let him go now he'll give the country over to ole Hitler straight away. I tell you I've *heard* him doin' it—telephonin' people an' tellin' 'em that the whole place was blown up jus' to scare 'em. He's got people workin' under him, too, same as he had in Norfolk. They were all telephonin' an' tellin' people the whole place was blown up jus' to scare 'em. They said that Marleigh police station was blown up. Well, that's a lie 'cause I passed it. An' Pithurst Lane an' Hill Road an——"

A light was slowly dawning in Mr. Balham's mind.

"Wait a minute, wait a minute," he said, giving his injured lip a reassuring final caress. "Where were you this morning when you heard all this?"

* * *

William walked slowly down the road homeward. Mr. Balham was an extremely patriotic little man, and he felt that William's zeal, though mistaken, was on the whole commendable. After dismissing the policeman, he had refreshed William with a large currant bun and a glass of lemonade and finally presented him with half a crown. Against his will, William had been persuaded of the innocence of his host. He was reluctant to abandon the carefully built-up case against him, but the currant bun and lemonade and half-crown consoled him. He decided to buy some new arrows with the half-crown. All his old ones, having found unauthorised marks of one sort or another, had been confiscated. He would go to the field behind the old barn with the Outlaws to-morrow morning, and they would have a bow-and-arrow practice. It was a long time since they'd had a bow-and-arrow practice. When he reached home, he found his mother still at work on the table napkins.

"Well, dear," she said, looking up from her work, "had a nice afternoon?"

"Yes, thanks," said William absently, wondering whether it wouldn't be better, after all, to buy water-pistols.

"What have you been doing?" went on Mrs. Brown.

William drew his mind with an effort from the all-important question of the half-crown (he must not decide in too much of a hurry; he could do with another boat; it was some time since they had had a regatta on the stream) to the details of an afternoon that was already vanishing into the mists of the past.

"Me?" he said vaguely. "This afternoon? Nothin' much. I caught that man you were all talkin' about this mornin', an' I was arrested for stealin' silver an' someone gave me half a crown."

Mrs. Brown was accustomed to her son's fantastic imaginary adventures.

"Yes, I'm sure you did, dear," she said. "Will you pass me the scissors?"

Chapter 2

William—The Highwayman

William walked down the lane towards the village, dragging his toes in the dust, his brows drawn together in their most ferocious scowl.

"Took off me!" he muttered fiercely. "Took off me jus' 'cause I rode on a plant. . . . Well, two plants. . . . Well, p'haps a few more. . . . Well, everyone's gotter *learn*, haven't they? I'd forgot how to do it an' I was jus' learnin' again. Jus' practisin'. Well, everyone's gotter *practise*, haven't they? Takin' things off people jus' for nothin' at all. Jus' for a few rotten ole plants that'd die nat'ral, anyway. Well, all plants die nat'ral, don't they?" he demanded aggressively of a cow that was gazing at him with large inquiring eyes over a gate. "Well, *don't* they?" he protested passionately.

The cow uttered a faint moo.

" '*Course* they do," argued William, taking the cow's attitude to be one of dissent. "Well, tell me one that doesn't, that's all. Tell me *one* plant that doesn't die nat'ral."

The cow was silent.

"*There!*" said William triumphantly. "I told you, didn't I? There isn't one that doesn't die nat'ral. They'd 've prob'ly died nat'ral to-morrow."

The cow mooed again.

"Oh, shut up," said William, turning away in disgust. "I'm sick of arguin' about it."

He continued, however, to enlarge on the theme as he went on down the lane.

"Prob'ly have died nat'ral by to-morrow. All this fuss jus' 'cause they had to pull 'em up a day before they'd 've had to do it anyway. . . . Jus' a few rotten ole plants. Takin' it off me for jus' a few rotten ole plants. An' stoppin' my pocket money till I'd paid for 'em. Stealin', that's what it is. They only come from seeds, plants do, don't they?"

He stopped to argue the point vehemently with a telegraph pole.

"Well, isn't seeds cheap enough? Jus' tell me anywhere you've not seen seeds a penny a packet." He uttered a short sarcastic laugh. "Sayin' they'd cost five shillin's when seeds is a penny a packet anywhere. An' hundreds of seeds what'd fill a whole garden. All for a penny. An' sayin' they cost five shillin's. Not so nice bein' stole off by your own family." He uttered a shorter and still more sarcastic laugh. "Not so nice to think of your own fam'ly bein' jus' storytellers an' stealers. . . ."

He remembered suddenly that Ginger, who had been staying with an aunt, would have returned home last night, and decided to go to him for sympathy.

"Bet if I was a grown-up I could get 'em put in prison," he muttered, turning into the lane that led to Ginger's house. "Bet I could. Bet they wouldn't dare steal off me if I was a grown-up. Bet——"

He suddenly saw Ginger walking towards him down the lane. His walk was, like William's, slow and dragging. He did not suggest a boy who has just returned from an enjoyable holiday.

"Hello," he said gloomily.

"Hello," said William.

"Has your bike come?" said Ginger, with a faint gleam of interest.

The cloud over William darkened.

"Yes," he said bitterly, "it's come all right."

"Where is it, then?"

"It's been took off me."

"Took off you?" questioned Ginger.

"Stole off me," William corrected himself.

"How?" said Ginger.

A mental vision came to William of his garden as he had left it—the flower beds criss-crossed with innumerable prints of tyres, the plants flattened to the earth. . . .

"I'd forgot how to ride," he admitted. "Well, I was only jus' learnin' again same as anyone might. Well, there's no lor against learnin' again, is there? You'd jolly well think there was, though, by the way they went on. . . . You can't stop it when you're learnin' an' it sort of goes where it wants. I'm black an' blue fallin' off, but they don't care about *that*. Oh, no! I don't s'pose they'd care if it'd killed me. All *they* care about is a penn'orth of rotten ole plants. Took my bicycle off me an' din't give me my pocket money. Just for a penn'orth of rotten ole plants."

Cheered by his own eloquence, he continued:

"Why, I bet cyclin' over that ground did it *good*, same as ploughin' or somethin'. Bet I saved 'em *trouble*, cyclin' over that ground. An' I bet everyone was sick to death seein' those ole plants day after day. They oughter be jolly grateful to me for knockin' 'em down so's they could put in a few new ones." He sighed deeply. "All grown-ups are mean, but I bet my fam'ly's about the meanest of the lot."

"I bet mine is," said Ginger gloomily.

"Why?" said William, slightly piqued by this challenge to his position as martyr-in-chief. "You've had a nice holiday an' I bet your aunt gave you a tip."

"Oh, yes," said Ginger bitterly. "Oh, yes, she gave me a tip all right. She gave me half a crown."

William's expression lightened somewhat.

"Well, come on, let's go 'n' spend it," he said simply. "It's the last bit of money I'm likely to see for a long time."

"Oh, yes, she gave it me, all right," said Ginger, "but I've not got it."

"Have you spent it already?" said William indignantly.

It was the unwritten law of the Outlaws that all tips should be pooled.

"Oh, no," said Ginger. "I've not spent it." His face clouded as at the memory of some intolerable wrong. "Well, that's what they're there for, isn't it?"

"What where for?" demanded William.

"It *says* they're there for a 'mergency," said Ginger vehemently, "an' if that wasn't a 'mergency I jolly well don't see what is. That's what I said to 'em an' they wouldn't listen. 'That's what they're there for, isn't it?' I said. 'Well, why d'you have 'em at all, then?' Wouldn't even let me get it. Went on at me 's if I'd murdered someone. Wish I had, too," he ended darkly.

"What happened?" demanded William.

"I keep *tellin*' you what happened," snapped Ginger. "Why don't you *listen*? I tell you, I dropped it an' pulled it an' they made as much fuss as if I'd murdered someone an' wouldn't even let me get out to look for it."

William considered this account in silence.

"*What* did you drop?" he said at last.

Ginger made a sound expressive of patience tried beyond endurance.

"What's the *matter* with you?" he demanded. "Why don't you *listen*? I keep tellin' you an' *tellin*' you. My half-crown, of course. What else could I drop? Jus' leanin' out of the window with it in my hand an' dropped it."

"What window?" demanded William.

Ginger looked at him helplessly.

"The train, of course. Jus' leanin' out of the train window with it in my hand an' dropped it. Crumbs! If that's not a 'mergency—well, I dunno what is."

Light dawned on William.

"Oh—an' you pulled that cord thing?"

" 'Course I did," said Ginger, "same as it tells you to. An', *gosh*, the fuss they made! Wouldn't even let me get down to look for it. An' a man came round to see my father about it las' night an' said they'd overlook it this time. Said *they'd* overlook it. I like that! It oughter be *me* overlookin' it. I bet I could've found that half-crown in two minutes if they'd let me look for it. . . . An' you should've heard the way my father went on at me about it. They oughter be made to give me another one. They've practically stole mine off me. Went on at me as if *I'd* done somethin' crim'nal, 'stead of them. What do they have 'em there at all for, if people can't use 'em? That's what I said to 'em. Or tried to say to 'em, but they wouldn't let me say anythin' at all. Jus' went on an' on at me. . . ."

"Jolly hard lines," said William absently, then re-turned to his own grievance. " 'Spose they'd all gotter learn themselves some time. I bet they ran over worse things than rotten ole flower beds."

" 'Spose they think it's jus' a nornament," said Ginger, with a sarcastic laugh. "Funny sort of ornament, that's all I can say."

"I bet they'd have died nat'ral in about a week."

"Why do they *say* 'For use in a 'mergency' if they don't mean it? That's what I said to 'em, but they wouldn't listen."

"Sooner than a week, prob'ly."

"Don't seem to understand English. . . . Don't know what 'mergency means, if you ask me."

"Ridin' over ground doesn't do it any harm. Does it good, same as rollin' the lawn. Always pickin' flowers themselves, but when I knock a few down, you'd 've thought the world had come to an end."

"It wouldn't 've taken two minutes to get down an' get it. Wouldn't 've taken me any time at all findin' it."

"I jolly well wish it *would* come to an end sometimes. I get nothin' but fusses made at me all day for doin' nothin' at all."

"Jus' the same as takin' half a crown off me. Same as highwaymen, they are. It's enough to turn me into a highwayman myself."

William considered this idea with interest.

"Gosh, so it is!" he said, and added, "I've often thought I'd like to be one."

"It'd serve 'em right," said Ginger. "It'd jolly well serve 'em right."

"I bet they have a jolly excitin' time, highwaymen," said William.

"There aren't any now," said Ginger. "They've died out."

"I dunno," said William vaguely. "I've heard people talk about highway robbery quite lately."

"Yes, but they only mean people chargin' too much for meals," explained Ginger, "not the old sort."

"There's no reason why the old sort shouldn't come back," said William. "I bet it only wants startin' again. . . . I'm sick of bein' gone on at 's if I was a murderer without the fun of murderin' anyone. There'd be a bit of point in bein' gone on at for bein' a highwayman if you'd been one. You'd sort of feel you'd got *somethin'* out of it."

"You've gotter have a black horse to be a highway-man," objected Ginger.

"You needn't," said William. "A bicycle'd do. If they'd not taken mine off me it'd have done fine. But we don't need anythin' like that really. We can run jolly quick an' that's all that matters. It's better not havin' a horse or a bicycle 'cause you can get away runnin' over fields an' things better."

Ginger considered the question again in silence.

"They've gotter have masks," he said at last.

"They needn't," said William, to whom the career of highwayman was beginning to seem not only attractive, but the obvious solution of all his problems. "I've seen pictures with crim'nals in, an' they jus' wear handker-chiefs over their noses. It's better than masks. It's not so old-fashioned."

"You've gotter have pistols," said Ginger.

"Well, we've gottem, haven't we?" said William impatiently.

"Only toy ones," said Ginger.

"Well, how're they to *know* they're only toy ones?" argued William. "They look the same as real ones. I bet they'll scare 'em same as real ones, so's they'll hand over their money an' jew'ls at once without waitin' to be shot."

"There aren't any coaches nowadays," said Ginger, "an' I bet cars won't stop for you, no matter how many handkerchiefs you have over your nose."

"All right," said William aloofly, "if you don't want to be a highwayman, don't be."

"I do," said Ginger, hastily climbing down. "I wanter be one same as you. Gosh! When I think of them stoppin' me gettin' down to get it when I'd took all the trouble pullin' it. I'll be one till I've got that half-crown out of someone, anyway."

"An' I'll be one till I've got the money they're goin' to make me pay for those ole plants," said William.

"Anyway," said Ginger, returning tentatively to his objection, "I bet cars won't stop for you."

"N-no," admitted William, "p'raps they won't. We'll have to find one that's broke down or waiting somewhere. . . . I don't say it's going to be easy, but it's worth tryin'. It's better than doin' nothin'. We could go up an' say 'Your money or your life', an' see what happened. I bet they'd be scared. If they weren't we could jus' run away. . . . All I want is money to pay for their rotten ole plants."

Ginger considered the question in silence. From being one of William's more fantastic and outrageous suggestions, the idea had suddenly taken its place in the world of possibilities.

"All I want is my half-crown back," he said.

"Come on, let's have a shot at it," urged William. "I'm sick of jus' bein' somethin' for other people to set on. I want to set on someone myself for a change. I don't mean go on doin' it all our lives same as people bein' doctors an' policemen an' suchlike. I mean jus' do it a bit till we've got back the money people owe us."

"Well," said Ginger, "I couldn't get into a worse row than I did over pullin' that thing. What's it *there* for, that's what I'd like to know. Why'd they *have* it if people aren't let use it? A normament, I suppose. Huh!"

"All right," said William, who was growing a little tired of Ginger's grievance. "All right. Well, we've gotter get handkerchiefs. I've got one somewhere. . . ." He dragged out a piece of fabric of indeterminate shape and colour. "I tore a bit off for somethin'—I've forgot what—but it'll be big enough. Doesn't matter it bein' a bit muddy. I used it dammin' a stream this mornin'.

Better, really, 'cause in the pictures they were black. Have you got one?"

Ginger burrowed in his pockets.

"No. . . . Gosh! I remember now. I was usin' it carryin' a frog I found. I think it's in the garden. . . . I'll get it—I won't be a sec."

"All right," said William. "Let's meet on the road just past the bus stop. It's nice an' lonely there. They always did it in lonely roads so's their cries for help wouldn't be heard."

"A' right," said Ginger. "Well, it'll teach 'em a lesson, anyway, an' they jolly well need it."

The two highwaymen met at the appointed place in the road just beyond the bus stop. They had agreed not to wear their masks on the way through the village, so as not to excite curiosity and comment.

"We won't put 'em on", William had said, "till we find a car to hold up. Then we'll jus' slip 'em on an' get out our pistols an'—an' hold it up."

The road was empty. They walked down it rather uncertainly.

"We needn't only do cars," said Ginger. "We could do people walkin'. I mean, there'd be two of us to only one of them."

"Y-yes," agreed William doubtfully. "Y-yes, but——"

The well-known form of General Moult was seen coming down the road.

"Quick! Come on!" said William. "Let's hold him up."

They slipped their handkerchiefs over their noses and stepped forward.

"Your money or your life," said William, holding out the pistol.

The handkerchief fell down about his neck as he spoke.

"What, what, what, what?" snapped General Moult, who was a little deaf, a little short-sighted, and more than a little irritable. "What are you talking about?" His eye flashed over Ginger, who still wore his handkerchief about his nose. "No, a very bad attempt at a guy. I shan't give you a penny. I'm surprised that you can't make a better guy than that. Besides, it's war time. No bonfires will be allowed in any case. Never heard of such a thing." He waved them aside with his stick. "Out of my way! Not a penny!"

They stared, looking after him.

"Well, *that* wasn't much good," said William. "He wouldn't even listen."

"Guy indeed!" said Ginger indignantly. "Guy indeed! I like that. I——"

"Look," said William. "Here's a motor-cyclist. Let's try him."

He pulled up his mask and stepped forward.

"Your money or——"

The motor-cyclist—a despatch rider in uniform—swerved and William fell back into the ditch. The cyclist cursed him furiously, then continued his meteor-like career.

"An' that wasn't any good," said Ginger.

But William, still in the ditch, was looking down the road.

"Come down here, quick!" he whispered. "There's a car comin'. . . ."

Ginger joined him in the ditch. The two watched while a car gradually slowed down till it came to a stop a few yards away from them. They heard a man say: Afraid I've run out of petrol. I'll walk back to the garage. It's not far. Now where are those coupons? . . . Oh, here!"

He seemed to be speaking to someone in the back seat

"YOUR MONEY OR YOUR LIFE," SAID WILLIAM, HOLDING OUT
THE PISTOL.

who was invisible to them. The person in the back seat
murmured agreement, and the man got out, slammed
the door, and set off down the road whistling.

William waited till he had turned a bend that hid him
from sight, then said, "Now!" in a short sharp whisper.

Mask firmly adjusted, pistol in his hand, he climbed
out of the ditch, flung open the rear door of the car and
said: "Your money or your life."

A little girl of about nine looked up at him in surprise.

"NO, A VERY BAD ATTEMPT AT A GUY. I SHAN'T GIVE YOU A
PENNY," SNAPPED GENERAL MOULT.

"What did you say?" she asked.

Though surprised, she was evidently not at all
perturbed.

"Why've you got those funny things on your faces?"
she asked.

"We're highwaymen," explained William, "an'
you've gotter give us your money, or we'll shoot you."

"Oh," said the little girl with mild interest. She put
her hand in her pocket and brought out three pennies.
"I've only got these. They're my pocket money."

William hesitated. His scheme had somehow not

included the taking of pocket money from little girls. He waved it aside.

"We don't want that," he said gruffly. He looked round the car and saw a suitcase on the floor. "Whose is that?"

"That's Uncle's," said the little girl, putting the threepence back into her pocket.

William lifted it experimentally.

"Gosh! It's heavy!" he said. "I bet there's treasure in it. Come on, quick, before he gets back." He fixed the little girl with a stern frown. "An' don't you tell him which way we went," he said, "or somethin' awful'll happen to you."

"What?" said the little girl.

"Never mind," said William darkly.

He began to lift the case out of the car.

"Are those handkerchiefs you've got over your faces?" said the little girl.

"Yes," answered William.

"What a horrible mess they're in!" said the little girl with disapproval. "I've never seen handkerchiefs in such a horrible mess. I hope your mother will be very cross with you for getting them into such a mess."

"I tell you we're highwaymen," snapped William. "We've not got mothers an' they're not handkerchiefs, anyway. They're masks. Now, remember, don't you tell him which way we went."

He plunged into the ditch and pulled the case through the hedge with Ginger's help. Together they lugged it across the field to the old barn.

"It'll prob'ly be locked," said William breathlessly. "We'll have to break it open."

"P'raps it won't be," said Ginger hopefully. "People often don't in cars."

"It's jolly heavy," panted William. "It's much too

heavy to be jus' clothes. Say! S'pose it's diamonds!"

"Or gold nuggets," said Ginger excitedly. "They're jolly heavy. . . ."

They dragged the case into the seclusion of the old barn's darkest corner and undid the straps.

"Bet it's locked," said William.

"Bet it isn't," said Ginger.

"Bet it is."

"Bet it isn't."

"Bet it—— Gosh! it *isn't*."

They tore it open, then stared at the contents. "Crumbs!" said William. "Jus' stones. Jus' ordin'ry stones."

They were, indeed, quite ordinary-looking stones about the size of cricket balls.

"They're certainly not diamonds," said Ginger with the air of an expert.

"P'raps they're nuggets," said William hopefully.

They took them to the door and examined them carefully. No, quite obviously, they were just ordinary stones.

"That's a nice way to treat highwaymen," said William in disgust. "Jus' a lot of dirty ole stones. Jus' a trick, that's what it is. Fillin' an ole suitcase with dirty ole stones."

"But they didn't know we were comin," said Ginger.

"N-no," said William, "but what were they doin' with a bag of dirty ole stones? P'raps they always keep it there for thieves. Jolly good idea," he admitted reluctantly, "keepin' a bag of ole stones for thieves to steal so's they won't take anythin' valu'ble. Bet that ole girl knew. I've a jolly good idea to go back an'——"

An idea suddenly struck him.

"*Tell* you what! Ethel's startin' a rock'ry. There aren't many dances now, 'cause of the war, so she's havin' a rock'ry instead. She said she'd pay me a penny each if I got stones for it. She wouldn't have the ones I found for her. Said they were the wrong shape, an' I got fed up an' said I wouldn't get her any more. We might try her with these. P'raps she'll give us sixpence for the lot. An' p'raps she won't" he ended morosely. "She's about the meanest of our family, an' *that* says somethin'!"

"It's worth tryin', anyway," said Ginger, bundling the stones back into the bag. "We'll pretend we took a lot of trouble gettin' 'em for her. Well, we did, come to that."

Ethel, it turned out, was in the garden, tending the budding rockery. It was an ambitious affair and so far had not progressed very far, as she was perhaps unduly particular about the quality of the stones she admitted to it. Perspiring admirers home on leave from Army, Navy and Air Force toiled up the hill and along the lane to the Browns' house, bent double beneath boulders of all shapes and sizes, only to be summarily dismissed with their burdens.

"It's no use," Ethel would say firmly. "I don't want just *anything*. The whole thing must be in *proportion*. Too large or too small isn't any use at all."

She had even taken a book called *Rock Gardening for Beginners* out of the Hadley Public Library and had read part of the introduction. Her conversation was full of such terms as "moraine", "pockets", "headlands" and "collars". The gardener had already given notice twice, and relations between him and Ethel were strained almost to breaking point.

It was, therefore, without much hope that William approached her with a specimen of his spoils.

"Would you like this for your rock'ry, Ethel?" he asked ingratiatingly.

Ethel threw it a careless glance.

"It's much too small," she said distantly. "I didn't say

I wanted *pebbles*." Then she looked at it more closely.
"Wait a minute," she said. "It's—— Where did you find
it?"

"Oh—jus' lyin' about," said William vaguely.

"It's rather uncommon," she said, "but it's so small
compared with the others." She closed one eye and
looked from the stone to the rockery with the air of an
expert deliberating some epoch-making judgement. "I
shouldn't mind a row of them on the top. It would be
rather ornamental. I think it would give it character.
Make it just a little different from the ordinary rockery.
But I don't suppose you could get any more like it."

"Yes, I could," said William. "I could get some more
all right. I—well, I did get a few more, case you liked it.
They're in the garage. I'll get 'em."

He fetched the other stones from the garage and laid
them out for her inspection. It would be just like Ethel,
of course, to change her mind at the last
minute. . . . But she didn't. She continued to regard
them with approval and interest.

"They *are* uncommon," she said. "I think they'd look
rather nice along the top. . . . I—I'll give you a penny
for the lot."

"Well, I *like* that," said William indignantly. "I jolly
well *like* that! A *penny* for—one, two, three, four—ten
stones. I've had all the trouble of gettin' 'em, an' you say
a *penny*."

"Well . . . twopence."

"No," said William firmly, encouraged by Ethel's
obvious desire for the stones, "I'm not lettin' 'em go for
twopence."

"Well, then sixpence," said Ethel reluctantly. "I'll
give you sixpence. Not a halfpenny more. If you don't
want sixpence, you can take them away."

"Oh, I want sixpence all right," said William hastily.

"You can have 'em for sixpence."

"I'll give it you to-morrow," temporised Ethel. "My bag's upstairs."

"I'll fetch it," said William. "I want it now or I'm not sellin' 'em."

"Oh, all right," snapped Ethel. "Anyone would think you thought I wasn't going to pay you."

"I've known you not," said William darkly.

When he came down with her bag she had arranged the stones at regular intervals about the top of the rockery. She handed him the sixpence, then stepped back to consider it, head on one side.

"Yes," she said. "It does give it character. . . . Where are you going?" as William set off towards the side gate.

"I'm goin' to give Ginger his threepence," said William. "He helped me—find 'em."

"There isn't time before lunch," said Ethel. "Mr. Durant's coming, and Mother particularly said you'd not to be late. I think he's here already."

"Mr. Durant?" scowled William who disliked the process of intensive cleansing that the presence of guests always necessitated. "Who's he?"

Ethel sighed.

"Don't you ever listen to *anything*?" she said. "We were talking about it all breakfast-time."

"I've got other things to think of at breakfast-time," said William distantly. "Who is he, anyway?"

"He's coming to lecture at the Village Hall this afternoon."

"What on?"

"Geology."

"What's that?

"Oh, do stop asking questions and go and get a *bit* of dirt off it you can. Your face is filthy."

"Huh!" said William. "I've got other things to think of than dirt. What about explorers? D'you think *they've* got time to wash their faces every other minute?"

"Well, you aren't an explorer."

"How d'you know I'm not?" said William. "I bet I'm a lot of things you don't know anything about."

"Oh, go and *wash*!"

"All right," said William with dignity. "I'm goin', aren't I?"

He entered the morning-room a few minutes later wearing the virtuous expression of one who has left no stone unturned in his search for cleanliness. He had, as a matter of fact, forgotten his hair, which stood up in wild confusion around his scrubbed and shining face. Mrs. Brown pressed it down as firmly and unobtrusively as she could while introducing him to the guest.

"This is William. . . . This is Mr. Durant, dear, who is going to lecture to us this afternoon."

William assumed the ferocious scowl that did duty as his "company" expression, shook hands with Mr. Durant, and muttered a greeting.

"And this", continued Mrs. Brown, "is his little niece."

It was then that William had his first shock. The little girl who had been in the car, from which he had taken the suitcase containing the stones, came forward, holding out her hand politely.

"I must apologise again for the niece," put in the lecturer. "She is staying with us and insisted on accompanying me."

"We're so glad she did," said Mrs. Brown. "William, dear, do try and look a little more pleasant."

Afraid of rousing her suspicions, William stretched his mouth to an inane grin and followed the company into the dining-room. It was evident that the little girl had not recognised him. He had, of course, been wearing his "highwayman's mask", and she had only seen his eyes and heard his voice. In order to prevent any possibility of recognition, he crossed his eyes and spoke in a shrill, high-pitched voice, as he asked Ethel for the salt. His mother looked at him helplessly, shrugged her shoulders, then turned her attention to the others.

"Mr. Durant says he lost a case of specimens on the way down here, Ethel," she said.

"Well, actually, it was stolen," said the lecturer. "I ran out of petrol and walked to the garage, and when I got back to the car the case had gone. My niece has a strange story to relate of it. She says that four masked highwaymen of immense stature came to the car and stole the case. One threatened her with a pistol and another said that he'd cut her throat if she stirred——"

"I never did," put in William indignantly.

They all stared at him.

"I mean," he stammered, "I mean, I'm jolly s'prised. I mean, 'Fancy that'! That's all I meant, sayin' 'I never did'. Same as Cook says 'Well, I never did'."

"He's mad," explained Ethel calmly to the guest. "Don't take any notice of him. He's not really dangerous."

"I suppose you've notified the police." said Mrs. Brown.

"Oh, yes," said the lecturer. "But I'm afraid that identification of the thieves will be difficult. You see, all my niece can tell me about them is that they're orphans and have dirty handkerchiefs."

"Well, they *told* me they were orphans," said the little girl, "an' I could *see* they'd got dirty handkerchiefs 'cause they'd tied them on their faces for masks."

"How odd of them to tell you they were ophans," said Mrs. Brown.

"The whole story's odd," said the lecturer mildly. "Why should they want to steal my specimens? And why four of them?"

"There may've been five," said the little girl. "They were very big an' *very* fierce. One of them had a dagger an' he said, 'Let's cut her head off,' an' the one with the gun said, 'No, let's shoot her,' an' another that had a piece of rope said, 'No, let's hang her,' but the other one said that I reminded him of his mother that was dead an' if they killed me they must kill him, too. An' that made them all think of their mothers that were dead an' they cried a bit with their dirty handerchiefs an' let me off. But they took the suitcase, 'cause they said they must do something."

"You're making all that up," said William severely.

"My niece's imagination is notorious," said Mr. Durant. "No doubt she has plentifully embroidered the facts of the case, but I'm afraid the main fact is true enough—namely, that my bag was stolen from the car while I went for petrol. Perhaps my niece got out for a little walk. . . ."

"Did you, dear?" said Mrs. Brown.

The little girl did not answer. She was staring at William with a curious expression. . . . His eyes reminded her of something, and at first she couldn't think what. His voice reminded her of something, and at first she couldn't think what. Then—but surely it couldn't be! She fixed him with an unflinching stare.

"They were *very* big men," she said aggressively, "an' there *were* four of them."

"A'right," muttered William, "I never said there weren't, did I?"

"William, William!" said Mrs. Brown reproachfully.

She had hoped that William would get on nicely with this dear little girl, but here they were quarrelling already about nothing at all. Odd the way they kept staring at each other, too. How funny children were!

"I do hope you can manage all right without your exhibits," she said to Mr. Durant.

"Oh, yes. More or less," he replied. "Of course, it makes it more interesting to have them."

"Are you interested in rock gardens?" said Ethel when they had finished lunch.

"Well, not particularly," admitted the guest.

"Oh, but you must see mine," said Ethel.

"It's a rotten one," put in William desperately. "An absolutely *rotten* one."

"William!" said Mrs. Brown again reprovingly.

It seemed to be one of William's bad days. He'd snapped at the little girl, and now he was snapping at everyone else. . . .

"I mean it's cold an' tirin' for him goin' out to see a rock garden," persisted William. "He'd much better rest quietly indoors. I'm thinkin' of *him*. I don't want him to get tired an' wore out lookin' at rock gardens before his lecture."

The little girl's eyes were still fixed on William in that challenging unblinking stare.

"Four big men," she said again. "An' one had a dagger an'—an' if that's your mother why did you say you hadn't got one?"

"Don't know what you're talking about," said William, returning her unblinking stare.

They had now reached the rock garden. William stood apprehensively on the edge of the group.

"This", said Ethel, "is a Mesembryanthemum."

But Mr. Durant wasn't interested in the Mesembryanthemum. He was interested in a stone about the size of a cricket ball. He had picked it up and was examining it.

"Where did you find this?" he said.

"My little brother found it," said Ethel. "And this is a Lithospermum."

But Mr. Durant wasn't interested in the Lithospermum either. He was still examining the stone.

"Most curious!" he was saying. "I'd no idea that there was any of this particular kind in this part of the country. But it's a bit of luck for me. If you'll kindly allow me to borrow it, it will be at least one specimen for my lecture."

"Certainly," said Ethel, rather impatiently, "and this is a Campanula tommasiniana."

But Mr. Durant had pounced excitedly upon another stone.

"Where on earth did you get this?" he said.

"My little brother found it for me," said Ethel. "This is a——"

"Where did he find it?" said Mr. Durant.

"Where did you find it, William?" said Ethel distantly, piqued by Mr. Durant's lack of interest in her rock plants. William turned his blank stare upon Ethel.

"Oh—jus' about," he said.

"My little brother roams the countryside far and wide with his little friends," explained Ethel. "Now this is a——"

"You found it in the immediate neighbourhood?" said Mr. Durant to William.

"Yes," said William quite truthfully. "I found it jus' outside the village."

"Most interesting," said Mr. Durant. "*Most* interesting. I must certainly make a note of that. It completely upsets the generally held theories on the subject. I must mention it in the book I'm writing, too. I——"

"*This*——" began Ethel firmly, but again she was interrupted, for Mr. Durant had pounced upon yet another of William's spoils. And another. And another. And another. . . .

"Would you," he said breathlessly, "would you kindly lend me all these for my lecture? They—they'll almost make up for the ones that were stolen from my car."

"I'm sure Ethel will with pleasure, won't you, dear?" said Mrs. Brown placidly. "But how will you get them to the Village Hall? I'll see if there's anything in the garage that will do."

She departed for the garage, leaving Mr. Durant staring from the heap of stones to William, from William to the heap of stones. Only Ethel seemed unaware of the tension of the atmosphere.

"*This*", she said, "is an Androsace lanuginosa."

Mrs. Brown returned, and William saw to his horror that she was carrying the very suitcase he had taken from the car.

"I've found this in the garage," she said. "I don't know whose it is. I believe it's an old one of Robert's. You know the sort of rubbish that collects in a garage when you haven't a car. Will it do?"

Mr. Durant stared at it till it seemed that his eyes must drop from his head. Then he found his voice and spoke as with a great effort.

"It will do excellently," he said. "Excellently."

Then he stared from one to another of them like a man in a dream. His gaze rested finally on William, and William's gaze flinched before it. . . .

"Well, we'd better go and get ready, Ethel," said Mrs. Brown, "or we shan't be in time to go with Mr. Durant to hear his lecture. We won't be long, Mr. Durant."

"He hasn't seen half my rock garden," said Ethel, plaintively. "He hasn't seen the Saponaria ocymoides. . . ."

She followed her mother indoors, leaving Mr. Durant with William and the little girl. William began to slope off, but Mr. Durant recalled him.

"I want a word with you, young man," he said.

Slowly and dejectedly William returned.

"Now," said Mr. Durant to his niece, "think very carefully. How many people were there who took that bag out of the car, and how big were they?"

The little girl pouted.

"Well, p'raps there weren't *quite* four," she said. "I'm not good at counting."

"And how big were they?" persisted Mr. Durant. "About as big as William here?"

"Well, p'raps not *much* bigger. I've got a very poor mem'ry. But", eagerly, "they *were* orphans. They said so."

"Never mind that for the present," said Mr. Durant. He turned his spectacled gaze on to William.

"And what have you got to say for yourself?"

It didn't seem any use to deny his exploit with the proofs of his guilt lying around him.

"Well, you see," said William, "I was sort of tryin' bein' a highwayman. They'd took my bicycle off me an' stopped my pocket money an' Ginger had lost his half-crown out of a train window so we thought we'd try bein' highwaymen. An' then when I found these were only stones I thought I might as well sell 'em to Ethel for her rock'ry an' get somethin' for 'em."

"I see. . . ."

At that moment the garden gate opened and Mr. Brown could be seen making his way up the drive. He had arranged to come home early in order to meet Mr. Durant and hear his lecture. He didn't like having to alter his day's routine, and his face wore the uncompromising expression of one who is going to stand no

"WELL YOU SEE," SAID WILLIAM, "I WAS SORT OF TRYIN' BEIN'
A HIGHWAYMAN."

nonsense from anyone. William's heart sank.

"That's your father, isn't it?" Mr. Durant was saying.
"I'll have a word with him on the subject."

Helplessly William watched him walk across to Mr.
Brown and enter into conversation with him. Crumbs!
This on top of the fuss about the bicycle. Gosh! What a
row there was going to be! Corks! Mr. Brown's lack-
lustre eyes were already roving round in search of him.

"Come here, William," he said shortly.

Despairingly, reluctantly, his mind a confused welter of unconvincing excuses, William approached the tribunal.

"Mr. Durant here has been talking to me about you," said Mr. Brown.

William's eyes went reproachfully to the lecturer, and he noticed for the first time that the eyes behind the spectacles were humorous and kindly. Sudden hope filled his breast.

"He says that you're interested in geology," said Mr. Brown. "I confess that I'm surprised. I didn't realise that you were interested in anything beyond making a nuisance of yourself. He says, would you and Ginger care to spend a day with him and his niece next week. You can see his specimens and—what else was it, Durant?"

"There's a very good film on," said Mr. Durant. "It's about highwaymen. I thought we might all go and see it together. . . ."

Chapter 3

Boys Will Be Boys

Consternation reigned in the Brown family when it was discovered that Mrs. Brown, slipping from the bottom rung of a ladder which she had been using to inspect her store cupboard, had broken a small bone in her ankle—a consternation that centred chiefly in William.

"If it weren't for William," said Mr. Brown.

"If it weren't for William . . ." said Robert.

"If it weren't for William . . ." said Ethel.

Even Mrs. Brown, lying pale and pain-racked, forbidden to put her foot to the ground, murmured feebly: "If it weren't for William. . . ."

William was amazed and outraged by their attitude.

"Me?" he said. "Gosh! I dunno what you mean. I jus' *dunno* what you mean. All I want to do is to help. All I *ever* wanter do is to help. You go on as if I was a *trouble*. I'm always tryin' to help."

"You're tellin' *us*," said Robert bitterly.

"Well, I am," said William. "I've wasted hours an' hours tryin' to help. . . . Well, I know it goes wrong sometimes, but it's never been *my* fault."

"No?" said Ethel, in what William mentally designated as her nasty tone of voice.

"Well, it hasn't," persisted William. "I've gone to no end of trouble tryin' to help ever so many times. I bet I can help now, all right, too. I can make cups of tea an'

things for her. I can sit with her an' talk to her. I can tell
her int'restin' things. . . . Well, I *can*. . . . I bet I know
a jolly sight more int'restin' things than what any of you
do. I bet——"

"That's enough, William," said Mr. Brown.

At a family conclave, from which William was
excluded, it was decided to send him away to any relative
who could be persuaded to take him.

"No one'll *want* him, of course," said Ethel bitterly.
"We'll have to make out it's a charity. Well, it *is* a
charity, of course. It's a question of Mother's life. It's
enough to kill any invalid just being in the same house
with him. . . . Who is there he could go to?"

"There's hardly anyone he's not been to," said
Robert, "and no one who's had him once is likely to want
him again. You can be pretty sure of that."

After an exhaustive survey of the Brown relations, it
was decided to write to Aunt Florence. Aunt Florence
was vague and notoriously short of memory. It was some
time since she had stayed at the Brown home, and, with
luck, might have forgotten what William was like.

Mr. Brown composed the letter that evening with help
from Robert and Ethel. He hinted darkly at further
possible complications in Mrs. Brown's ankle and
implied that William had undergone a change of heart
since Aunt Florence had last seen him. ("He's very
much looking forward to seeing his aunty again," he
added untruthfully, at Ethel's suggestion, in a P.S.)

"Though I don't suppose it'll have any effect," said
Ethel gloomily, "not if she's any memory at all. I mean,
even one minute of William is a never-to-be-forgotten
experience."

William was torn between a desire that his honour
should be vindicated by an enthusiastic invitation from
Aunt Florence and a reluctance to leave home.

"I bet she'll want to have me," he prophesied with confidence. "I bet she'd *enjoy* havin' me. Anyway, I don't want to go. I keep tellin' you there's things I could do to help if you'd let me stay here. I could help Cook——"

"Yes, you helped Cook yesterday, didn't you?" said Ethel sarcastically.

"Oh, that," said William evasively. "I'd almost forgot that. Well, listen. I di'n't mean to eat it all. I only meant to taste it. Well, I like that stuff they make cake out of, an' it was sort of all gone before I re'lised it. An' the fuss she kicked up!"

"I don't wonder," said Ethel. "One would hardly believe that even *you* could have eaten up a whole bowl of cake mixture just while she'd gone to the door to take the bread from the baker."

"Well, I keep tellin' you I di'n't *mean* to eat it all," protested William. "I only meant to taste it. Well, I di'n't know I *had* eaten it all till I sud'n'ly saw it'd all gone. An', gosh! I might've *murdered* someone, the way she carried on!"

"And you're surprised that no one wants to have you."

"I bet they do," said William. "I bet they'd *all* want to have me, if you gave them a chance. I'm not any trouble at all. I'm a *help*. . . . I bet you anythin' she'll want to have me."

And, sure enough, there arrived a letter from Aunt Florence the next morning saying that she would have William. It was not an enthusiastic letter. It breathed the spirit of one who had never yet failed in a disagreeable family duty and who was not going to fail now. . . . It expressed the hope that Mrs. Brown's ankle would soon be quite well.

"Told you so," said William triumphantly. "Told you

she'd want to have me, all right."

"She doesn't say she wants to have you," Ethel pointed out.

"No, but I bet she means it," said William. "I bet she means it, all right. I bet she only didn't say it 'cause she di'n't want to waste paper with a war on and she thought you'd know she meant it . . . but, anyway, I don't want to go away. I—I"—he searched for a reason that would appeal to the adult mind—"I don't want to miss school."

"If that's worrying you," said Mr. Brown, "I'll ask your aunt to see that you do a few lessons each day."

"No, that's all right," said William hastily. "No, that's quite all right. . . . I mean, p'raps it would be good for me to have a holiday from lessons. I've been feeling a bit overworked lately."

And with that he retreated in good order, leaving them too astounded to reply.

He set off to Aunt Florence's the next day. As both Robert and Ethel refused to take him, he had to travel alone. The journey was fairly uneventful. He annoyed an old gentleman by playing on a mouth-organ that he had brought with him to while away the time, and an old lady by passing continually from one window to the other, always treading on her toes on the way and never failing to apologise profusely. On one occasion he leant so far out of the window that he nearly overbalanced and had to be hauled back to safety by the combined efforts of the entire carriage.

Aunt Florence was at the station to meet him. She did not fail to notice the look of relief on the faces of his fellow travellers as he leapt exuberantly out on to the platform, followed by his suitcase, which he had forgotten and which the old gentleman threw out after him with what seemed unnecessary violence. Aunt Florence greeted him with a somewhat strained smile.

THE OLD GENTLEMAN THREW OUT
WILLIAM'S SUITCASE WITH WHAT
SEEMED UNNECESSARY VIOLENCE.

"I hope you're not going to be a nuisance, William,"
she said.

William stared at her in blank surprise.

"Me?" he said. "Me a nuisance? I never *am* a
nuisance. I'm a help. I'm always *tellin'* people I'm a help.
Why, they didn't want me to come away 'cause I'm such
a help, but I'd got a bit overworked an' they thought a
holiday'd do me good."

It was Aunt Florence's turn to stare at him in blank surprise.

"You don't *look* overworked," she said at last, "and your father didn't say anything about it in the letter I had from him."

"No," said William, "he didn't want to worry you. An' the way I look now's the way I look when I'm overworked. When I'm well I look the same as other people look when they're overworked."

Aunt Florence considered this in silence for some moments and finally gave it up.

"Well, I shall be very busy while you're here," she said, "and I shan't be able to go about with you much. I hope you'll be able to entertain yourself."

"Oh, yes," said William, much relieved by this news. "Oh, yes, I'll be able to entertain myself, all right. I'm jolly good at entertaining myself."

The next morning he sallied forth to inspect the neighbourhood. It was a very small village. Its chief interest and almost its only topic of conversation was the Flower Show that was to be held at the end of the month. And that, less because of any interest in the show itself than because of the rivalry of two old men who had shown fruit and vegetables there for the past fifty years and whose rivalry had grown deeper and more venomous with the passing of each year. At first they had shown all kinds of exhibits with varying success, but of late years their rivalry had crystallised into a furious contest for supremacy in hot-house peaches and asparagus. It was a neck and neck race. All that the rest could hope for in these two classes was a third place. For the last four years, Colonel Summers had won the first prize for peaches and Mr. Foulard for asparagus, and each longed with all his heart and soul to beat the other in his speciality. Mr. Foulard tried to find out how Colonel

Summers treated his peaches, and Colonel Summers tried to find out how Mr. Foulard treated his asparagus, but each preserved the utmost secrecy, often going out under cover of darkness to give doses of his pet fertiliser, so that no rumour of it could reach the other. Last year once more Colonel Summers had won the first prize for peaches, and Mr. Foulard for asparagus, and this year each had inwardly vowed to win the first prize for both. . . .

All this William gathered in a stroll round the village. In the sweetshop the general opinion was that Colonel Summers would win the first prize for both peaches and asparagus. In the post office, on the contrary, the majority seemed to hold that Mr. Foulard would win them both, while in the grocer's the more conservative element seemed to predominate and predicted that Colonel Summers would yet again win the first prize for peaches and Mr. Foulard for asparagus. . . .

After listening to these conversations, William had formed a distinct mental picture of the two men. He imagined Colonel Summers round and pink and peach-like, and Mr. Foulard tall and thin and asparagus-like. It was, therefore, something of a shock to discover that Mr. Foulard was round and pink, and that Colonel Summers was tall and thin and, from long sojourn in the East, of a yellowish-green complexion. Both passed the post office while William was there.

"Look! There's old Summers. Thinking about his peaches, I reckon, by the smile on his face."

"Look at old Foulard out for his constitutional. They say he was messing about with his asparagus till after midnight last night."

And William looked at the tall spare man and the little tubby one with that interest that his fellow creatures never failed to evoke in him.

After doing the errands with which his aunt had commissioned him in the village, he set out on a tour of the countryside, enlivening it as usual with sundry imaginary adventures. It was while he was engaged in pursuing a tribe of Red Indians, whom he had put to flight alone and unaided, that he ran into a man just entering a pair of impressive iron gates. He ran into him with such violence that he ricocheted backwards, fell full length on the ground, then found himself looking up into the yellow-moustached face of Colonel Summers.

"Well, well, well, well!" said Colonel Summers. "Where are you off to in such a hurry?"

"Nowhere," said William, scrambling to his feet. "I mean, I'm just walkin' along same as you."

Colonel Summers laughed.

"Well! Well! Well!" he said again. "I don't think I know your face, do I?"

"No," said William. "I've come to stay with my aunt. I got a bit overworked an' needed a holiday . . . an' my mother'd sprained her ankle," he added as an after-thought.

"Well! Well! Well!" said Colonel Summers. He looked at William's dust-covered figure. "You'd better come in and have a brush-down. You can't go back to your aunt in that state."

Nothing loath (for in William's eyes any adventure was better than none), he accompanied the tall lank figure up the drive and into the big white house at the end. Inside the hall, the Colonel took a clothes brush from the hatstand and gave William a perfunctory brush-down, then led him into a room hung round with various Eastern weapons.

"I dare say you'll be interested in these, my boy," he said, and proceeded to describe them in detail, with many somewhat lengthy anecdotes. He spoke with the zeal of one who finds a new and unexpected audience. It was easy to guess that the stories had been told so often that their narrator now found it difficult to get anyone to listen to them. And William was a most satisfactory audience. He listened open-mouthed. He examined the weapons with eager delight. He was particularly interested in some Burmese knives in painted leather sheaths.

"Perhaps I'll give you one of those before you go," said Colonel Summers.

He was in high good humour. It was years since he had told the stories except to the accompaniment of strangled yawns, and expressions of acute boredom. William was a godsend to him. . . .

"Look in again some time," he said genially, as he saw him off at the side door and pointed out a short cut to the village through the kitchen garden. "Yes, look in again and we'll have another yarn. . . . And don't forget, I may give you one of those knives before you go. . . . Shut the gate after you."

On his way to the gate William passed a large hot-house, where the famous peaches were ripening, but his mind was too full of Burmese knives and tigers and snakes and hostile tribes to have much thought to spare for peaches.

He was a Burmese with a knife in a sheath of painted leather. . . . He crept along under the shelter of the wall, his hand on the handle of the knife, then leapt forward among his enemies, engaged in a desperate hand-to-hand fight and pursued them in wild disorder down the road. One of them, however, seemed suddenly to stand his ground and resist, seemed even to attack William ferociously in return about the head and ears. . . . Coming back to reality, William became aware of the red angry face of Mr. Foulard just above his own.

"I hope that'll teach you to look where you're going,"
he was saying as he administered a final cuff. "Disgraceful! Charging into people like that! You deserve to be
handed over to the police, you young ruffian!"

Then he strutted angrily in at a gate that bore the
inscription "Uplands".

The next morning William called on Colonel Summers again. And the next. And the next. Colonel
Summers remained pressing in his invitations. Strangely
enough, it was William who began to weary. He heard
the same stories in the same words with the same
gestures over and over and over again . . . and irresistible sleepiness began to creep over him. Colonel
Summers' repertoire was a large one, but he worked it
hard. The minute he'd finished, he began again. He had
a loud, grating voice that began to wear down even
William's iron nerves. If it hadn't been for the Burmese
knife William would have stopped going after the second
or third round of the stories. But he wanted the Burmese
knife, and he shrewdly judged that he was expected to
earn it by providing Colonel Summers with an audience.
But, of course, even the thought of the Burmese knife
couldn't occupy his mind all the time, and he began to
take more and more interest in the peaches. His
footsteps lingered as he passed the hot-house on his way
to the side gate. Often the door was shut. Often, too, a
gardener was there—a morose man who received all
William's overtures of friendship with stone-like im-
mobility. There came a morning, however, when the
door was open and the gardener absent. . . . William
looked round. There was no one in sight. The temptation to go in and examine the peaches at closer quarters
was irresistible. It couldn't do any harm, he assured
himself, just to go in and *look* at them. He wouldn't
dream of touching them. . . . He went in and examined

them with interest. Their velvety texture fascinated him. It couldn't do any harm, he assured himself, just to *touch* one. He wouldn't dream of eating any. He stroked one softly. At least, he meant to stroke it softly but, to his consternation, the stalk snapped and the peach fell on to the ground. . . . He gazed at it, at first dismayed, then interested. . . . Well, he might as well *eat* it. . . . In fact, he'd better eat it, then no one could come along and find it lying there and make a fuss. A pity it had come off, but now it had come off the only thing to do was to eat it. Interesting to see what it tasted like. He didn't think he'd ever had a peach. . . . It was the sort of thing grown-up people gave other grown-up people when they were ill. . . . No one ever gave *him* anything but castor-oil when he was ill.

He sank his teeth into the soft flesh, and in a moment it had all disappeared, leaving only a circle of juice and a blissful smile on his mouth. It was *jolly* good. He'd never had anything quite so good. Better than doughnuts or bull's-eyes or even strawberry ice. He looked at the massed peaches all around him. They'd never miss just one more. Actually, he thought, there were far too many. He remembered the gardener's spending an afternoon "thinning" apples and gooseberries at home. It would be a kindness to thin these peaches a bit. They jolly well needed thinning. Probably ole Colonel Summers would be grateful to him. Probably he'd meant to do it himself and had forgotten. The best ones hung high overhead, but a ladder was conveniently set up against the top branch. He climbed up . . . took a peach and ate it . . . took another . . . and another . . . He had forgotten everything in the world but the delicious taste of peaches. He was, in fact, nothing but a living, breathing lust for peaches. . . . Suddenly he heard a loud shout and the sound of running footsteps. He dropped a half-eaten peach and looked round. The gardener and Colonel Summers were running towards the hot-house, their faces livid with fury. . . . Obviously William's presence had been reported, probably by one of the maids. The two were out for vengeance. Panic-stricken, William slipped, and the ladder went from under him, crashing through the glass. Instinctively he grabbed at the nearest bough to save himself. There was a shower of peaches and the sound of wrenching as the supports gave way and the whole tree came down. The Colonel and his gardener gazed on the scene of destruction, paralysed with horror. But the paralysis did not last long, and as one man they fell upon the unfortunate William crawling from under the debris. . . .

Five minutes later he limped painfully out of the gate, bruised by his fall, but still more by the heavy hand of Colonel Summers' gardener. Colonel Summers himself had been too distraught to do much more than dance a sort of dance of anguish round his ruined peaches, but the gardener had swiftly secured William and laid on good and hard.

"Gosh!" muttered William as he limped along the road. "Gosh! I wonder there's any of me left. Well, I di'n't *mean* to. It wasn't my fault. It must've been a rotten ladder. . . . Well, I di'n't eat many. I can't help people havin' rotten ladders. Mus' have been a rotten tree, too, to come down soon as I caught hold of it. . . . 'Tisn't as if I'd eaten many. I'd not had time to eat many. Jus' came down soon as I touched it. . . ."

He slackened his pace apprehensively as he neared his aunt's and rehearsed his story under his breath.

"Well, I hardly *touched* it. . . . It jus' came down all of a sudden. Must've had some disease. Same as elm trees, comin' down sudden with some disease on top of people. I'd only *jus'* touched it. Well, a *tree* didn't ought

to come down jus' with *touchin'* it. . . . I prob'ly saved
his life with lettin' it come down on me 'stead of him. He
ought to be grateful to me. . . ."

It wasn't a very convincing story, but he hoped he'd
have time to perfect it before Colonel Summers came
round to complain. As he opened the garden gate he
comforted himself by the assurance that there wouldn't
have been time for Colonel Summers to come and
complain yet. . . . He would probably still be dancing
his dance of anguish round his tree. But, though Colonel
Summers had not been in person to complain, he had
telephoned. And—much to William's regret, for he'd
taken a lot of trouble over it—his story was not required.

"I don't want to know what happened, William," said
his aunt firmly. "Colonel Summers rang up to ask for
your father's address, and I've given it to him. He's going
to write to your father and make his complaint and
demand damages. No, I don't want to know why he
ought to be grateful to you. He certainly didn't *sound*
grateful to you. . . . I don't want to hear anything more
about it. Colonel Summers is going to write to your
father, and I don't consider myself called on to take
steps, though I'm very sorry to hear that you've
disgraced yourself. . . . Now go and wash. You're in a
shocking state. Your face is covered with dirt."

"It's not dirt," said William morosely. "It's bruises.
It's a wonder I'm alive. I was jolly nearly killed.
. . . What with rotten trees fallin' on me an' madmen
settin' on me. . . . Well, he *mus'* be mad. Stands to
reason he mus'. . . . Settin' on people like that just
'cause a rotten tree fell on 'em. You ought to be jolly
grateful I'm alive," he ended pathetically.

His aunt preserved a speaking silence, so he went
slowly upstairs, groaning loudly on each step, and
waiting hopefully for sympathetic question or comment.

None came. Once round the bend of the stairs he leapt fairly nimbly up to the bathroom. . . .

He decided to go out for a long walk in the afternoon. His aunt obviously didn't want him indoors, and he could no longer go round to Colonel Summers' house to hear his non-stop stories of the East. The Burmese knife was definitely off. He was sorry about that, but not altogether sorry about the cessation of the non-stop stories of the East. . . . His thoughts began to turn to his own generation. He hadn't seen any of them about except a fat pale boy about the same age as himself, who, accompanied by a fat pale mother, went for the same walk through the village and along the main road every afternoon. He had heard the mother address the boy as "Georgie", but, beyond a spirited exchange of grimaces whenever they met, contact had not been established. He hadn't many hopes of him, but at least he was a boy. . . .

He set out in the opposite direction from Colonel Summers' house and wandered aimlessly along the road. He felt depressed by the events of the day. Colonel Summers would probably have written to his father by now, giving him (as William considered) a wholly untrue account of the accident. He wondered whether to write to his father himself and complain of having been injured by the falling of a rotten peach tree and then cruelly assaulted by its owner, but, remembering his father, he decided that it would be a waste of time. . . . Well, he wasn't going home for another week, so nothing could happen to him for another week. Perhaps if he behaved very well, his aunt would ask him to stay longer, and his father would have forgotten Colonel Summers' letter by the time he got home, but, remembering his aunt, he didn't think that this was likely to happen. His gloom increased. . . . Suddenly, at a bend in the road, he came upon "Georgie" and his mother.

"Hello!" said William in a propitiatory manner. He felt pathetically alone in the world—an unusual thing for him—and would have liked even this fat pale boy for a friend. The mother looked at him with an expression of disdain, and Georgie flung him a grimace containing such unmistakable malice that William was for a moment taken aback. He returned it in a half-hearted fashion and walked on despondently. Suddenly a large stone hit him in the middle of his back. He swung round

GEORGIE'S MOTHER TURNED AND BORE DOWN UPON WILLIAM, HER FACE RED WITH ANGER. "YOU *WICKED* BOY!" SHE SAID.

in time to see Georgie standing in the attitude of one who has just thrown a stone, a malicious grin on his fat pale face. His mother was looking down at him tenderly and saying: "Don't get your hands dirty, darling." Then they turned round and continued their walk. William, stung into retaliation, stooped down, picked up the stone and flung it back. It hit Georgie neatly in the neck. He broke into a howl of rage. . . . His mother turned and bore down upon William, her face red with anger.

"You *wicked* boy!" she said.

"He threw it first," William justified himself. "He——"

"HE THREW IT FIRST," WILLIAM JUSTIFIED HIMSELF.

But she was a large woman and by now was almost on him, so William, choosing the better part of valour, took to flight.

The incident depressed him still further. The whole world seemed to be against him. . . . Rotten trees falling on him . . . madmen attacking him . . . and now this awful fat woman and Georgie. . . . And for no reason at all. . . .

Passing the gate of Uplands he saw Mr. Foulard approaching it from the other direction. Another of these madmen who attacked on sight. The place was full of them. "More like a lunatic asylum than a village," muttered William bitterly. . . . He was giving him a wide berth when he saw that Mr. Foulard was smiling at him amiably across the road, displaying two large gold back teeth. William stared at him in amazement.

"And how's my young friend?" Mr. Foulard was saying with obviously friendly intent.

William scowled, suspecting mockery or a trap, but Mr. Foulard was taking a handful of coins out of his pocket, was picking out two half-crowns, was handing them to William and saying heartily:

"I suppose a little pocket-money never comes amiss? Unless boys have changed since my time, what?"

"Th-th-th-th-thanks," stammered the bewildered William as he took the two half-crowns.

He couldn't think what had happened since yesterday. What had happened since yesterday was that Mr. Foulard had heard of the destruction of his rival's cherished peach tree, and was delighted by the now certain prospect of winning the first prize for both peaches and asparagus. He felt grateful to William as the means by which Providence had accomplished this miracle. In the first rush of feeling he had thought of giving him ten shillings, but discretion had prevailed.

"Had tea?" went on Mr. Foulard jovially.

William shook his head. He was past speech.

"Come along, then," said Mr. Foulard, waving his podgy little hand towards the gate of Uplands. "Come along! What about a piece of plum cake? Plum cake never comes amiss to a boy, what?"

He led William up the short drive and in at the door of the house, beaming down at him affectionately. The boy who had done in ten minutes what he'd been trying in vain to do all these years, knocked out old Summers and his peaches. . . . He patted his head as they entered the house.

"Now we'll see about that piece of plum cake, eh?" he said.

It was while William was just finishing a hearty tea that he got his next shock. Hearing voices outside, he looked up and saw Georgie and his mother passing the window.

"Ah, my daughter and little grandson," said Mr. Foulard. "You haven't met them, have you?"

"Er—yes," said William slowly. "Yes, I've met 'em, all right. I met 'em this afternoon."

"Splendid, splendid!" said Mr. Foulard. "I'll go and tell them you're here."

He went out of the room, and William sat staring fixedly at the door, a half-eaten piece of plum cake in his hand. Scraps of conversation reached him.

"Not *that* boy!" came in the fat woman's voice, up-raised indignantly. "Not that *dreadful* boy! The one that wrecked poor Colonel Summers' peaches?"

"Boys will be boys," came genially in Mr. Foulard's voice. "Boys will be boys, you know. We mustn't be too hard on them."

"And he threw a stone at Georgie."

"Dear, dear!" said Mr. Foulard. "That's bad, but——"

He was evidently torn between a desire to champion the destroyer of his enemy's most cherished hopes and a fear of his formidable daughter.

"Boys will throw stones, you know," he went on. "Perhaps he didn't see him."

"*See* him?" said Georgie's mother indignantly. "He threw it *at* him. Georgie had just thrown a little one gently at him in play, and then this great bully took up a big one and threw it as hard as he could. He made poor Georgie cry, didn't he, darling?"

"Yes, Mother," came in Georgie's fat slow voice.

"Well, my dear," said Mr. Foulard deprecatingly, "I can't just turn him out. After all——"

After all, he meant, I shall owe my first prize to him.

But Georgie's mother brushed him aside and entered the room, fixing a cold stare on William.

"Good afternoon," she said icily.

"Good afternoon," said William.

Something told him that his meal was to be abruptly terminated, so he hastily swallowed what remained of his plum cake as he returned her greeting.

"You've finished your tea, haven't you?" said Georgie's mother, and without waiting for William's spirited denial (there were some ginger biscuits that he hadn't even touched) continued: "I'm sure it's time you went home."

"I thought perhaps he might have a little game with Georgie before he went home," suggested Mr. Foulard mildly.

"Certainly not," snapped Georgie's mother. "I should never allow Georgie to play with a great bully like that. I can't think why you asked him in at all. What's your name?"

"William Brown," said William indistinctly through the last mouthful of plum cake, at the same time slipping one or two of the ginger biscuits into his pocket. (After all, he had definitely been asked to tea, so he considered that he'd a right to them.)

"Then you'd better go home at once, William Brown," said Georgie's mother. "And don't ever come here again. I can't think how you had the impudence to come here at all after the shocking way I saw you behave this afternoon."

"I didn't know you lived here," said William with spirit, "or I wouldn't have come. I don't want to play with any silly ole cry baby."

"How *dare* you!" said Georgie's mother, advancing upon him, while Georgie screwed up his face for another howl, and Mr. Foulard shrugged helplessly in the background.

"All right," said William. "All right, I'm goin'. . . ."

He scraped the crumbs on his plate carefully together, put them into his mouth, and withdrew with as much dignity as he could muster.

Georgie unscrewed his face into a sly smile. He had thought of a plan for increasing the discomfiture of his enemy. (He regarded all other boys as enemies on principle.) It was a plan that he had used with success on many previous occasions. A nice handful of mud flung from some reliable cover within easy reach of the house and his mother. . . . This boy would have to go down the drive to the front gate. He would take up his position behind the laurel bushes that bordered the drive. . . . Chuckling to himself, he slipped out of the french window. William did not hurry. He had never been in this garden before and probably would never be in it again. He might as well do a little exploring. . . . He wandered off the drive, took a look at the famous asparagus bed, then began to make his way slowly towards the front gate. Suddenly a handful of mud struck him on the side of the face, filled his mouth and eyes, and ran down his collar. He had a vision of a fleeing figure and leapt to the pursuit. Georgie had made a slight mistake. He had been expecting William to appear in front of him in the drive and, when he appeared on the other side of the laurel bush, had still flung his handful of mud without realising that his way of retreat to the house was cut off. He fled as quickly as he could, hardly knowing where he was going till he reached the asparagus bed. There, as it happened, William caught him up, and dealt him a powerful blow on the nose that sent him sprawling among the cherished shoots. Normally Georgie was a coward, but the pain of the blow turned him into a small inhuman fury. William was a small inhuman fury to start with. Boys in this condition have little sense of property. The two did not even realise that they were fighting on an asparagus bed at all, much less on a bed of prize asparagus watered by the sweat of Mr. Foulard's brow and fed, metaphorically speaking, by his tears. They plunged and reared and trampled and leapt and wrestled. Georgie's madness sustained him only for about five minutes . . . but by the end of those five minutes the battle-ground was a muddy stew, garnished with a few asparagus stalks. When the mist of fury cleared from before his eyes and he realised that a nasty rough boy was hitting him as hard as he could, he turned and ran back to the house with howls of rage. William stood gazing around . . . and gradually the full horror of what had happened dawned on him.

"Gosh!" he said aghast. "Gosh! Seems as if I couldn't go anywhere or do anythin' without messin' up people's prize stuff. Well, this wasn't my fault. No one could say this was *my* fault. . . ."

THEY PLUNGED AND REARED AND TRAMPLED AND LEAPT AND WRESTLED.

But apparently someone could and did. When William reached his aunt's house, it was to find that Mr. Foulard had rung her up to demand his father's address. He was going to write at once to lodge his complaint and demand compensation for his asparagus bed.

"Well, it wasn't my fault," said William. "Honest, it

v

my fault. He threw mud at me, an'—well, we got
in'."

His aunt looked at him helplessly.

"I simply can't understand it, William," she said.
"Can't you *move* without damaging people's property?"

"I wish you'd listen," said William. "I tell you the
boy——"

But she cut him short.

"I don't want to hear anything about it," she said.
"Mr. Foulard is dealing direct with your father, just as
Colonel Summers is doing. I really don't know *what* your
father will have to pay for a valuable hot-house full of
prize peaches, and a bed of asparagus."

William was silent for a minute, then said:

"When was I s'posed to be goin' home?"

"At the end of next week," said his aunt with a wistful
sigh.

William's visit had seemed a very long one—longer
even than she had thought it would.

William considered the prospect of homecoming. His
father would, of course, have received both letters of
complaint by then. He tried to picture the resultant
interview with his father. . . . Imagination and heart
alike failed him.

"I—I don't mind stayin' a little longer jus' to keep you
comp'ny," he said tentatively. "I—I could do lots of
things to help you, if you'd like me to stay a bit longer."

"You haven't done anything to help me yet," said his
aunt coldly.

"No, but I will," he assured her. "I will, hon-
est. . . . You tell me what to do, an' I'll do it. I—I'll help
in the house. I've always wanted to clean windows. I
bet——"

"*No*, William," said his aunt with a shudder. "You'll
go home at the end of the week as arranged."

"Haven't you enjoyed havin' me?" said William pathetically.

"No," said his aunt simply. "I didn't expect to. I took you because your mother had sprained her ankle."

"Oh . . ." said William and after a moment's thought added bitterly: "Funny thing my father never seems to get any illnesses. Funny when you think of all the people ill all over the world an' my father never gettin' anything."

His mental picture of an enraged parent had become so unpleasantly vivid that he decided to go out for a walk and try to forget it. But here again was a difficulty. To go in one direction would take him past Colonel Summers' house, and to go in the other would take him past Mr. Foulard's. To neither of them would the sight of him be welcome at the moment. He decided to go past Colonel Summers' and to dodge back at once if he met him. He groaned inwardly as he saw Colonel Summers issuing from the front gates just as he was passing them and was preparing to dodge back, when he saw that Colonel Summers was beckoning to him in an undeniably friendly manner. He approached cautiously.

"Well, well, well, well!" said Colonel Summers. "What about that knife? D'you still want it?"

Colonel Summers had only just received the news of the destruction of his rival's asparagus bed, and his heart was full of gratitude to William. Things were, at any rate, evened up. He could bear the loss of his peaches now that old Foulard had lost his asparagus, too. Moreover, he was a kind-hearted man and somewhat regretted the display of fury to which he had treated William. . . . He remembered, in his own boyhood, climbing a ladder to steal his grandmother's peaches. After all, he thought, boys will be boys. . . . He had kept putting off writing the letter of complaint to William's father, and decided now not to write it at all. Poor old Foulard! What a bait he'd be in! He'd been so sure of his first prize for asparagus. Poor old Foulard! One couldn't help smiling at the thought.

"I'm going away till to-morrow," he said genially to William. "Come in for it to-morrow morning. And about that letter. . . ."

"Yes?" said William hoarsely.

"Well, on the whole, I've decided not to send it. . . . Boys will be boys. . . . Well, come for your knife to-morrow."

And he went on down the road, leaving William staring after him in amazed relief. . . . He'd get the knife, after all . . . and there'd be only one letter of complaint to his father instead of two. One was bad enough, but it was better than two. . . . And he'd have the knife. And, he assured himself, he'd made things fair. They would get a prize each. . . . If nothing else happened, of course. . . .

But something else did happen. It was as if fate simply couldn't leave him alone. . . .

William was wandering down the road that evening, his heart full of gratitude to Colonel Summers. In a censorious and misunderstanding world, the Colonel seemed his only friend. When, therefore, passing the Colonel's house, he saw a red glow through the trees, he thought it best to go and investigate. Perhaps one of his outhouses was on fire. He could not omit this small service to his only friend. . . . He pushed the gate open and went to where he had seen the glow. It was all right. It was merely the remains of a garden fire. Relieved, he went out and home again, leaving the gate open. . . .

It happened that every night at about this time Farmer Jones' cattle were driven from field to farm. They knew the road blindfolded. But never before had the gate of

Colonel Summers' garden stood wide open like this. Farmer Jones had stopped in the field to repair a haystack, so the cattle were left to their own devices. There is an unsuspected element of adventure in cattle. They love to explore any unaccustomed avenue. . . . They poured in at the gate of Colonel Summers' garden.

The news reached Mr. Foulard just as he was writing the letter to William's father, complaining in highly coloured language of the destruction of the asparagus bed. He was demanding ten pounds' compensation. He was describing William as a Hun and a Goth and a Vandal. Then the news came. Colonel Summers' asparagus bed had been turned into a ploughed field overnight. Someone (no one knew who) had left the gate open, and twenty-five cattle had apparently danced the hornpipe on it. There was not a vestige of asparagus left. He laid his pen down, and a slow smile spread over his face. Poor old Summers. Peaches *and* asparagus gone. What a state he'd be in! He saw in his mind's eye the published results of the show. "Mr. H. B. Foulard— Hot-house Peaches—1st Prize." And poor old Summers nowhere. . . . What he'd been working for all these years had simply dropped into his hands like—like a ripe peach. He chuckled at the apt simile and began slowly to tear up his letter to William's father. Boys will be boys, he said to himself. No need to be too hard on the little blighter. If it hadn't been for his messing up old Summers' peaches he wouldn't be in the position he was in now—sole winner of first prize, with old Summers nowhere, for the first time in the history of the show. The little blighter had made a mess of his asparagus bed, but probably Georgie had done his fair share of damage, though his mother had insisted most indignantly that her little angel was incapable of hurting a fly, much less an asparagus bed. Anyway, he felt much too pleased at the turn affairs had taken to put any real spirit into letters of complaint. He'd go and have another look at his precious peaches. Wouldn't old Summers dance with rage when they got the first prize! . . . "Mr. H. B. Foulard—Hot-house Peaches—1st Prize." Ha, ha!

The next morning William made his way, rather warily, to Colonel Summers' house. He felt a bit scared, but, after all, Colonel Summers had definitely promised him the knife, had definitely asked him to call for it this morning. And if he had to hear all those stories of the East again—well, it was worth it. He wanted that Burmese knife more than anything else in the world. But Colonel Summers was definitely not in his Stories-of-the-East mood. He received William coldly. He did not know that William was responsible for the wreck of his asparagus bed, but the wreck of it had brought back his earlier grievance about the peaches. His mind's eye saw those same fatal words that Mr. Foulard's saw: "Mr. H. B. Foulard—Hot-house Peaches—1st Prize." And inwardly he raged and gnashed his teeth. It was all this wretched boy's fault. If it hadn't been for this wretched boy, at least he'd have had his peaches.

"The knife?" he said distantly. "What knife?"

"The—the knife you promised me," stammered William.

"I think you must have misunderstood me," said Colonel Summers. "I admit that I once intended to give you a knife, but; if you think over what's happened since you came here, you'll realise that you can hardly expect me to give you one now."

"Well, I've done all I could to make up," pleaded William.

"What have you done?" asked Colonel Summers.

"Well, I'd've put out a fire if there'd *been* one las'

night. I came in 'cause I *thought* there was a fire an' I wanted to put it out for you. . . . I di'n't know it was only a garden fire when I came in. I *meant* to put out a real one for you."

Colonel Summers' face was turning from its usual yellowish white, to pink . . . to brick red . . . to purple. He rose and stood threateningly over William.

"So-it-was-*you*-who-left-the-gate-open?" he said between his teeth.

William quailed. He realised that he'd given himself away irrevocably. He'd hoped that his contribution to that particular escapade had escaped detection. After all, he had told himself, he hadn't *done* anything. It wasn't *his* fault that Farmer Jones' cows went into people's gardens. He'd even tried to persuade himself that he had shut the gate and that they had opened it themselves. Well, animals *did* open gates . . . he'd read about it in books. . . . They were jolly intelligent, animals were.

"But listen . . .," he pleaded desperately. "Listen . . . I din' know——"

At that moment the door opened and a housemaid entered with a letter on a tray.

Colonel Summers took it up, his hand still trembling with rage, and read it. It was from the Committee of the Flower Show, saying that, owing to war conditions, the show would not be held this year. A slow smile spread over Colonel Summers' features. Saved! Saved from ignominy at the eleventh hour! He wouldn't get any first prize, but neither would that worm Foulard. Smack in the eye for that worm Foulard! Wipe the smirk off his face. The thought of the smirk on Mr. Foulard's face had been tormenting Colonel Summers all morning. Yes, old Foulard had thought he was going to put it over him at last. He imagined old Foulard reading the letter. Ha, ha! Snooks for him! Snooks for old Foulard!

He became aware of William looking up at him in surprise as his expression changed from rage to relief, from relief to triumph. (Poor old Foulard, foaming at the mouth! . . . poor old Foulard, thinking his rotten little peaches were going to get a first prize!)

"Well, well, well, well!" he said, smiling down at William (perhaps the little devil had left the gate open but, after all, boys will be boys. . . . One mustn't be too hard on them). Poor old Foulard! His one and only chance of getting first prize for his rotten little peaches gone for ever. He'd like to see the blighter now— foaming at the mouth. In its way, it was quite a good joke. "What was it you came for? A knife, wasn't it?"

"Y-y-yes," stammered the bewildered William. He didn't know what to make of it. Mad at you one minute and giving you knives the next. He'd better make the most of the giving-you-knives minute before it changed back to the mad-at-you. . . . "Yes, you said you'd——"

"Of course, of course," said the genial Colonel Summers. (Little devil, of course, but so were all boys. . . . He'd been a little devil himself once. Boys will be boys. Poor old Foulard. Ha, Ha! Poor old Foulard!) "Now you can take your choice, my boy. I'll give you any one of them you like. . . ."

* * *

It was the evening of William's return. He had gone upstairs to wash after the journey. Mr. and Mrs. Brown were sitting downstairs waiting for him.

"Odd those letters we had from Florence," said Mr. Brown reflectively, "saying that William had done something dreadful and that I should shortly be receiving appalling bills for damages from a Colonel Summers and a Mr. Foulard.

"I suppose you may still get them," sighed Mrs. Brown.

"I don't think so. My experience is that people write letters of complaint at once or not at all."

"We'd better ask William when he comes down," suggested Mrs. Brown.

"A lot of information we'll get from him!"

"We could write to Florence," said Mrs. Brown.

Mr. Brown raised a hand in protest.

"Eleven years' experience as William's parent, my dear," he said, "has taught me to let sleeping dogs lie."

At this point William entered. He looked shiningly clean and innocent.

"Well, did you have a nice time at your aunt's?" said Mr. Brown.

"Yes, thanks," said William, sitting down and taking from his pocket a comic that Aunt Florence had bought for him to read on the journey. (One of the things William could not understand about grown-ups was that they seemed to imagine one could waste the precious hours of a railway journey in reading.)

"Anything exciting happen?" said Mrs. Brown.

William considered.

"No," he said at last. "Nothin' really excitin'."

"Let me see," said Mr. Brown thoughtfully, "there was a Mr. Foulard there, wasn't there? Did you have anything to do with him?"

William opened the comic and looked at his father impassively over the top of it.

"Him?" he said, as if searching in the recesses of his memory. "Oh, yes. He gave me five shillin's an' invited me to tea."

"And what about Colonel Summers?" said Mrs. Brown.

William put down the comic and brought the Burmese knife from his pocket.

"Yes, he was jolly nice, too. . . . He gave me this."

Mr. and Mrs. Brown looked at each other and shrugged helplessly.

Chapter 4

William—
The Fire-Fighter

William and the Outlaws were thrilled to find that an Auxilliary Fire Service "area" had sprung up overnight in Hadley. At least, it wasn't there when they went into Hadley one week, and it was there the next. It appeared suddenly in a garage on the outskirts of the town, complete with trailers, pumps, and a heterogeneous collection of cars. Added to this were miles of hose-pipe and a glorious spate of water. All behind an imposing erection of sandbags.

The Outlaws could not tear themselves away from the fascinating spectacle. God-like beings in long rubber boots reaching almost to their waists waded about the swimming garage floor, polished the trailers, tinkered with the cars and did physical jerks. Occasionally they sallied forth with cars and trailers to neighbouring ponds, where they detached the trailers, unwound the hoses, and sent breathtaking sprays of water in every direction.

Forgotten were all the other interests which had once filled the Outlaws' lives. They now went down to Hadley Garage immediately after breakfast and stayed there till it was time to go home for lunch, returning immediately afterwards to stay there till tea-time. A house at the back of the garage was used as cook-house, dining-room and dormitory. Savoury smells came from it. Roars of laughter came from the dining-room when the god-like beings assembled there for meals.

At first the Outlaws contented themselves with watching this paradise through the gates. Then, cautiously, they entered and hung about just inside. Nothing happened. No one took any notice of them.

It was William who first dared to give a hand with a trailer that a small man with a black moustache was cleaning. The small man seemed to accept his presence and his help as a matter of course, even addressing him as "mate", which made William feel dizzy with rapture. The other Outlaws followed. . . . No one objected to them. Some of the men even seemed pleased to dally in their work to talk to them and explain the various contraptions to them. One of them let William hold a hose-pipe.

"I don't see why we sh'u'nt join 'em prop'ly," said William to the Outlaws as they went home, drunk with pride. "Well, we *helped*, din' we? I bet we'd be jolly useful to 'm. I don't see why we sh'u'nt join prop'ly."

"We've not got uniforms," Ginger reminded him.

William dismissed this objection with a sweeping gesture.

"They don't matter. Anyway, they've only got those A.F.S. letters on ordin'ry suits. We could easy get a bit of red cotton an' put A.F.S. on ours."

"I bet they wouldn't let us join," said Henry.

"Well, we needn't 'zactly ask 'em," said William. "We'll jus' go same as we did to-day, an' do a bit of helpin', and they'll get used to us gradual till they won't know we weren't part of 'em right at the start."

The others continued to look doubtful.

"The little one was jolly nice to us," went on William. "I bet they'll all be nice to us once they get to know us."

"I've known people not be." Douglas reminded him.

"I bet these will be," said William, the optimist. "I bet they'll be jolly grateful to us. Anyway, I vote we jus' go an' join 'em to-morrow an' do all the things they do. We'll have badges same as them an' I bet they'll think we've been part of 'em all along. We'll make the badges of red cotton——"

"We've not got any red cotton," said Douglas.

"Well, we can get some, can't we?" said William irritably. "Goodness me! You all go on an' *on* makin' objections. I bet I find some in Ethel's work-box. She's got every poss'ble colour of cotton there is. . . . Anyway," firmly, "we're part of the A.F.S. now, an' we'll go there to-morrow morning an' do all the things they do. . . . I'll go'n' have a look for the red cotton now."

He found the red cotton (or rather silk) by the simple process of turning out the contents of Ethel's work-box on to her bedroom floor and rummaging among them till he found it. Then conscientiously he bundled everything back and was much aggrieved by Ethel's reproaches later in the day.

"Well, I put 'em *back*, din' I?" he said. "Well, they looked all right to me. . . . I put 'em *back*. Well, I'd *gotter* have that red cotton. . . . No, I can't tell you why. . . . It's somethin' to do with winnin' the war. . . . No, I can't tell you what it is. . . . The Gov'ment says we mustn't go talkin' about things we're doin' to win the war. You don't know where ole Hitler is, listenin'."

He took the reel of red silk to the old barn and also a needle that he had thoughtfully purloined at the same time.

"It'll be quite easy," he said. "You jus' sew A.F.S. on, an' I bet it'll look same as theirs."

A few moments later he doubtfully surveyed the

spidery network of red threads that he had made on his coat.

"Well, anyway," he said, "you can see it's meant to be A.F.S. if you look close enough. It's a jolly good A and the F's not bad, an' I bet the S doesn't matter so much. Well, stands to reason you can't do a letter like S with an ordin'ry needle. I bet they have special ones."

With frowning concentration each of the others outlined spidery hieroglyphics on his coat. They, too, inspected the finished results doubtfully—results more suggestive of laundry marks gone mad than a badge of Government service.

"They're not bad," said William. "They're red, anyway, an' it doesn't matter what the 'zact letters are. Well, we'll be with the real ones, so people'll know it's meant to be A.F.S."

Wishing to give an impression of good discipline, he marched his band through the main street of Hadley the next morning and then boldly in through the garage gates. It happened that the A.F.S. was drawn up for parade. They stood stiffly in a row, their backs to the gate, waiting for the Section Officer to appear through the door of what had once been the motor sale-room.

William marched his band up to the end of the line, where they took their places, standing straight to attention. At that moment the Section Officer appeared at the doorway. His eyes swept down the ranks of the men to rest finally upon the Outlaws. . . . His face darkened. He was a youthful platinum blond, with an exaggerated idea of his own importance. He couldn't tolerate anything that made him appear ridiculous, and he considered that the presence of the Outlaws at his firemen parade made him appear ridiculous.

He bore down on them furiously.

"Get out of this at once!" he thundered. "How dare

you come in here! Don't you know that you're trespassing?"

"Yes, but——" began William.

Section Officer Perkins was large and muscular and he looked like business.

"All right," muttered William hastily, and withdrew with his Outlaws in as good order as possible.

Outside he turned to them.

"Well, I like that!" he said indignantly. "I jolly well *like* that. I bet he's no right to go turnin' people out of the A.F.S. I bet he'd jolly well get into trouble if the King knew that he was goin' about turnin' people out of the A.F.S. I've a good mind to write and tell him——"

"When we've took all that trouble over our badges, too," said Ginger gloomily, looking down at the vague and spidery red threads that adorned his coat.

"Let's wait till he's done an' then go in again," suggested Henry.

William shook his head. Despite his youth he was not without judgement and had spent many years of his short life gauging how far one could go with grown-ups of various types. He judged—quite rightly—that, for the present at any rate, it wasn't safe to go any further with that particular young man.

"No, let's go home," he said. "I'm sick of the rotten old A.F.S. Let's go'n play Red Indians——"

They went home and played Red Indians, but somehow all the glamour had faded from the game. None of them could put any conviction into it. It wasn't real any longer. Only the A.F.S. was real.

"Tell you what," said William finally. "We can go'n watch 'em same as we used to. . . . We can do that, at any rate. He can't stop us goin' to watch 'em same as we used to. . . . An' we'll keep our badges. He can't stop us havin, badges. . . . They might all fall ill sudden or get

"GET OUT OF THIS AT ONCE!" THUNDERED THE SECTION
OFFICER. "HOW DARE YOU COME IN HERE! DON'T YOU KNOW
THAT YOU'RE TRESPASSING?"

burnt up in a fire, an' then I bet they'd be jolly glad to
have us."

They went down to Hadley the next morning and took
up their old position outside the A.F.S. station, their
noses glued as usual to the bars of the gate. But evidently
not even that was to be allowed them. Section Officer
Perkins espied them, recognised them, and bore down

WILLIAM HAD MARCHED HIS BAND UP TO THE END OF THE
LINE, WHERE THEY TOOK THEIR PLACES, STANDING STRAIGHT
TO ATTENTION.

on them, his face flushed with the memory of yesterday's
affront to his dignity and with secret apprehension of
another.

"Clear off at once, you boys!" he said. "I won't have
you hanging about like this. If I find you here again, I'll
hand you over to the police."

Reluctantly the Outlaws drifted away.

"Well," said William with rising indignation. "I like

that. I jolly well *like* that. The street's not his, is it? The whole place isn't his, is it? Who does he think he is? Lord Mayor of London or Hitler or what? Let's go back there. Gosh! He can't stop people *lookin'* at him, can he? He'll have to make himself invisible if he's goin' to stop people *lookin'* at him. Crumbs! That's a new lor, that is, that people aren't allowed to *look* at people. . . I bet there'll be a jolly lot of accidents," he went on sarcastically, "with people runnin' into each other an' such-like, now people aren't allowed to *look* at each other. . . . Corks! That's a jolly funny lor, that is!"

"Let's go back there, then," said Ginger.

But William was reluctant to go back. It wasn't a question of the law. Grown-ups, as William had learnt by bitter experience, were a law to themselves. William was a brave boy, but not one to court disaster unnecessarily.

"'S no good," he said gloomily. "He'd only come an' make us go away again. I've met people like him before. Tyrunts same as the ones in hist'ry. Ole Stinks at school's one. Well, come to that, all schoolmasters are. They're all tyrunts, same as the ones in hist'ry. An' this ole Section Officer's another. I shouldn't be surprised if he's a schoolmaster in disguise. You can't mistake' em, but—well, I'm not goin' back there. I 'spect he wishes we would. I 'spect he'd jolly well like us to, but I'm not goin' to. . . . Tell you what. . . ." A gleam of inspiration flashed into his face. "*Tell* you what. We'll have one of our own. Well, he can't stop us doin' that, can he? He can stop us joinin' his, but he can't stop us havin' one of our own. We'll have a sep'rate branch, an' I bet we put out more fires than what his does.

"It'll be a bit difficult, won't it?" said Ginger thoughtfully.

"Course it won't," said William stoutly.

"We've not got a trailer nor a hosepipe nor anythin'," said Douglas.

"Corks!" groaned William. "You can't do anythin' but make objections. I never saw anythin' like you. We c'n get a wheelbarrow—can't we?—an' a hose from the garden an' we've got our badges an' that's all we need. We'll do all the same sort of things they do, an' we'll know when there's a fire 'cause we'll see them goin' to it, an' we can go along an' help, an' I bet we can put out fires as well as what they can—or a jolly sight better. You only need *water* for puttin' out fires an' water's cheap enough, isn't it? An' there's no *lor* to stop anyone what wants to puttin' out a fire, is there?"

His eloquence was, as ever, convincing, and the Outlaws gradually found themselves becoming convinced.

"We've gotter have a place to be an A.F.S. in," objected Henry feebly, "an' the ole barn's too far away. We sh'u'n't know what they were doin'."

"Course we can't use the ole barn," said William. "It's miles away. We've gotter stay joined to the A.F.S. here. We're *part* of the A.F.S. here, whether ole Monkey-face wants us to be or not. I bet he'll be jolly glad of us before we've finished."

"Yes, but what about a place?" persisted Henry.

"There's that bit of empty ground nex' the garage," said William. "That'll do for us, all right."

There was, indeed, a small plot of waste ground next to the garage and on this the Outlaws took up their position the next morning. They had a wheelbarrow in which was a bucket of water, a length of hose and a garden syringe that Henry had "borrowed" from the toolshed.

It was of an up-to-date kind and had a little contraption at the end of a length of tubing that you dropped into the bucket of water and that enabled you to spray out the whole of its contents without dipping the nozzle into the water. The gardener, the apple of whose eye it was, had been called up recently, and Henry was hoping for the best.

"I'll get into an awful row, though, if my father finds out," he said.

"Well, *goodness*!" said William, indignantly. "You'd think that winnin' the war came before squirtin' a few roses an' such-like, wouldn't you? Well, it seems a bit more important to *me*, anyway. Funny thing to think squirtin' a few roses more important than winnin' the war. I bet your father could get put in prison for thinkin' that."

"Oh, well," said Henry mildly, "he's jolly busy jus' now so p'raps it'll be all right. What'll we do first?"

"We'll see what they're doin' an' do that," said William. "Go 'n' see what they're doin', Ginger."

Ginger went to peep through the gates of the garage.

"They're doin' drill," he said when he returned. "Ole Monkey-face is drillin' 'em."

"All right," said William. "We'll drill too."

For the rest of the morning William's band of A.F.S. followed the procedure of the mother branch next door. Ginger was sent round at frequent intervals to report any change in the programme.

"They're cleanin' the trailers now."

And at once the Outlaws set to work upon the wheelbarrow, turning it upside down and dusting it with handkerchiefs already so grubby from various other activities that a little dirt more or less made no difference.

"They're squirtin' their hose now."

And at once the Outlaws took down the bucket of water and set to work with the garden syringe. Fortunately it was only a short walk out of the town to refill the bucket at a convenient roadside ditch.

Passers-by looked with amusement at the four boys busily intent on imitating their neighbours, but the Outlaws were too much occupied to have any time to spare for passers-by. . . . If Section Officer Perkins knew of this caricature of his dignified proceedings taking place on the other side of the garage wall, he gave no signs of it. His face still wore its expression of portentous self-importance.

At the end of the day William was well satisfied with the progress made by his band.

"We've done all the things they've done," he said, "An' we've done 'em jus' as well—or a jolly sight better. We'll come again to-morrow, an' I bet we'll soon be beatin' 'em hollow."

Their ardour was unabated next morning, and they took up their position on the piece of waste ground.

"P'raps they'll be doin' somethin' a bit different to-day," said William hopefully.

Ginger, sent to reconnoitre, brought news that they were preparing to fix trailers on to the cars.

"They're goin' out somewhere," he said. "I bet they're goin' up to Lengham ponds."

"All right," said William, in his most business-like manner, "we'll go there, too. Get everything ready quick."

In a few moments the A.F.S. cars came out of the garage, occupied by Section Officer Perkins and his band, the trailers attached.

At once William and his company emerged from the piece of waste land, wheeling the wheelbarrow, complete with bucket of water, length of hose and syringe. Section Officer Perkins turned to glare at them, then drove on furiously.

"Well, of course," said William as the cars vanished into the distance, "we can't keep up with them. We're

to keep up with them. But I bet they're goin' to
Lengham ponds. We'll go there anyway an' see."

They trundled their way through the town, spilling a
good deal of water and rousing much amusement among
the onlookers.

"Bet they're at Lengham ponds," William kept
saying.

And there, sure enough, they were. They were
putting one end of a hose into the pond and directing
water from the other end at various spots indicated by
Section Officer Perkins. As the Outlaws appeared, they
were just beginning to pack up the trailers to return
home.

The Outlaws trundled their barrow down to the pond,
took out their syringe, and, under William's direction,
squirted a thin stream of water at the A.F.S.'s latest
target, a tall, thin birch tree on the edge of the pond. It
was, perhaps, unfortunate that Section Officer Perkins
happened to be passing behind the birch tree.

The thin stream of water hit him full in the eye as he
turned round. . . . He strode towards the Outlaws, his
face white with anger, and William, realising the
inadequacy of his forces to deal with the situation, led a
hasty retreat into the surrounding wood.

"He's jealous, that's what he is," he said, as, having
watched the departure of the rival band, he returned to
the wheelbarrow, still carrying the precious syringe.
"He's jealous 'cause we're as good as what his lot are."

"He was mad 'cause that water hit him in the eye,"
said Ginger, putting the facts of the case more simply.

"Well, goodness me!" said William. "Fancy a fireman
mindin' a bit of water in his eye. Corks! A fireman's
gotter get used to bein' *soaked* all over. Jus' shows what a
rotten fireman he is," he ended with satisfaction. "I
knew he was a rotten fireman soon as I saw him.

Anyone'd be a rotten fireman with hair that colour. Stands to reason."

The routine of drilling and cleaning the wheelbarrow soon began to pall, and William's plans of emulating the canteen by making a fire on the piece of waste land and cooking a mixture of cold sausage and roly-poly pudding (purloined from the larder) in an old saucepan (purloined from the dustbin) was nipped in the bud by a passing policeman.

To make matters worse, Section Officer Perkins developed a new technique. He came and watched the Outlaws with a sneer of superior amusement. He brought his friends to sneer at them. He once deliberately directed the hose over the wall of the garage so that William was soaked from head to foot. Fortunately, William's mother was out when he reached home, and his vague explanation, given on her return, of having "got into a bit of water" was accepted with the inevitable "William, you are dreadful! What *will* you do next?"

"What we've gotter do", said William, addressing his band the following morning, "is to find a fire 'fore they do, an' put it out. *That'll* show 'em, all right. They'll treat us a bit diff'rent after *that*. Jolly snooks for them, comin' along after we've put the fire out. Come on. Let's go an' have a look for a fire."

Refilling the bucket at the ditch, testing the syringe to make sure that it was in working order, giving the wheelbarrow a final dust over with their handkerchiefs, the Outlaw A.F.S. sallied forth in search of a fire.

They went through the main streets of Hadley, inspecting each house and shop carefully, without result.

"Gosh!" said William at last, irritably. "You'd think with all these people there'd be a fire *somewhere*. To see 'em throwin' down matches an' cigarette ends all over the place you'd think there'd be no end of fires. Can't think what *happens* to 'em all."

They abandoned the main streets at last and began to roam the smaller back streets, still inspecting each house carefully for signs of a conflagration.

"Wouldn't do 'em any harm to let us have a little one," he muttered pathetically. "*Mean*, I call it."

"Well, they don't *want* fires," Ginger reminded him mildly.

"No, but—well, you wouldn't think a *little* one'd do 'em any harm. I mean, when you read of all the fires there are in the newspapers it seems sort of *mean* of 'em to start bein' careful just when we're lookin' for one."

"S'pose we couldn't start one ourselves," suggested Douglas.

William shook his head.

"No," he said reluctantly. "That wouldn't count. We've gotter find one."

"Look!" said Ginger excitedly, pointing to a small back window. It was open a few inches at the top, and from the opening swirls of white vapour were pouring out.

"That's smoke! That's a fire!"

William stopped, set down the wheelbarrow and looked at it with the air of an expert.

"Yes, that's a fire all right," he said.

He advanced and made a closer inspection through the window. Nothing could be seen but the thick eddies of white vapour.

"It's cert'nly a fire all right," he said again.

The four Outlaws stood gazing in at the window.

"Can't see any flame," said Henry.

"Course you can't," said William. "It's right inside the house, the flame is. We've gotter fight our way through the smoke to the flame. We've gotter tie handkerchiefs over our mouths an' fight our way through the smoke same as the real ones do. There's probably people unconscious inside, overpowered by the fumes, same as there are in the newspapers, an' we've gotter rescue 'em."

"Won't we let the others help at all?" said Ginger, somewhat appalled by the magnitude of the task that lay before them.

"Oh, yes, we'll send 'em a message about it," said William, "an' we'll let 'em come along an' help, but we'll start on it alone first jus' to *show* 'em. We'll prob'ly 've put it out an' rescued all the people by the time they get here."

A small boy in spectacles was passing along the street. William called to him.

"I say," he said. "Go'n' tell the A.F.S. at Hadley Garage that there's a fire at"— he glanced at the number of the street —"10, Nelson Street, and tell 'em to come quick."

"All right," said the boy, and he set off with unexpected agility in the direction of the garage.

"Now we've gotter put wet handkerchiefs over our faces," said William, "an' get the syringe thing full and then fight our way in through the smoke. Ginger 'n' me'll put out the fire, an' Henry an' Douglas can rescue the people. I 'spect they'll be unconscious. I 'spect you'll have to squirt water on 'em and drag 'em out. . . . It's jolly dangerous an' I 'spect that other lot of A.F.S.'ll get here too late to help. I 'spec we'll get medals or somethin'."

It took longer than they thought to adjust the wet handkerchiefs. At last they were ready, however, and armed with syringe and pail of water, headed by William, they marched up to the door.

William flung it open.

Clouds of white vapour enveloped him. Almost at the same time a door into the room from the house side opened and the figure of a woman entered. They could see it dimly through the thick vapour. Ginger pointed the syringe at it and squirted. He explained afterwards that his whole mind was set on squirting and somehow he couldn't help squirting at the first thing he saw move.

The woman gave a loud scream. It was a scream of anger and indignation. It was definitely not the grateful scream of someone being rescued from a fire. Instinctively the Outlaws drew back, and at that moment the A.F.S. from Hadley Garage arrived. The messenger had been a fleeter runner than he looked and had met them at the gate just starting out, completely equipped, for a mobility exercise. They had driven straight to the address given them by the spectacled small boy. Section Officer Perkins appeared at the door. Behind him was a fireman holding the nozzle of a hose, the other end of which was being attached to the nearest hydrant.

With the opening of the door the atmosphere was gradually clearing. It showed a kettle boiling vigorously on a gas ring. It showed a large woman, standing arms akimbo and glaring angrily at Section Officer Perkins. Her face was dripping with water from Ginger's syringe, but somehow that did not detract from the awful impressiveness of her appearance.

"How *dare* you!" she thundered.

"I—I beg your pardon," stammered Section Officer Perkins.

"I said 'How *dare* you!'"

"I—I—I don't know what you mean!" spluttered Sections Officer Perkins. "I—I——"

"I shall report you to headquarters," went on the woman. "As if I hadn't got enough trouble to-day. First that girl puts the kettle on and forgets all about it for over half an hour." She turned and switched off the gas with a sudden vicious gesture. "Gas bills mean nothing to *her.* . . . And then you and your lot coming larking along. Let me tell you, young man, I can take a joke as well as anyone, but I don't call this a joke. I've heard of your sort and I think it's time a stop was put to it. You've chosen the wrong house to come to with your tom-fool tricks and I shall report you to headquarters this minute. Larking into respectable folk's houses and turning your hosepipes on to them."

"I—I never turned the hosepipe on to you," protested the Section Officer indignantly.

"Am I wet or am I not?" demanded the woman, turning her portly person to him for his inspection. There wasn't any doubt at all that she was wet. Her hair was wet, her face was wet, her ample bosom was wet. "And", she went on without waiting for his answer, "you've got the impudence to say you never turned the hosepipe on me."

"I—I—I never did!" said Section Officer Perkins again.

"Funny thing, isn't it?" she said sarcastically.

The steam had now mostly found its way out or hung in beads of moisture on walls and ceiling of the little spick-and-span scullery. "Funny thing to come in here, and get a squirt of water in my face and then look round and find you standing there with your hosepipe. You ought to be ashamed of yourself. A man of your age larking about like a schoolboy! You deserve the sack and I hope you get it."

"Madam," said the Section Officer desperately, aware of his firemen sniggering behind him, "I protest. I got a message that there was a fire here and I came along."

"That's a nice tale," said the woman. "Who sent the

message and why need you start squirting me in the face the minute you get here?"

Section Officer Perkins looked round. There was no one there but his own A.F.S. squad. William had long ago quietly withdrawn his band under cover of the steam before anyone had realised their presence.

"I can't understand what happened," he said. "A boy brought a message that there was a fire here and we were needed at once, and, as for turning on the hose, the very idea's ridiculous."

"So *you* say," said the woman darkly. "I prefer to believe my eyes. And now that's enough of your sauce, young man. Off you go or you won't be the only one throwing water in people's faces. Off you go and take your grinning monkeys with you. I've got work to do if you haven't."

With that she pushed him back and slammed the door in his face. Section Officer Perkins drove slowly back to his station. His face was set and stern. He looked like an extremely dignified young man whose dignity has been sorely affronted. As he passed the piece of waste ground next to the garage he drove very slowly indeed, fixing his gaze intently on William and the Outlaws. They were, however, engaged on the innocent task of cleaning the wheelbarrow with the air of having been hard at work on it all morning.

Section Officer Perkins went into his office looking thoughtful.

As soon as the A.F.S. had disappeared through the garage gates, William laid aside the handkerchief, with which he had been making a pretence of polishing the wheels, and heaved a sigh of relief.

"*That*'s all right," he said. "Gosh! I was afraid they'd 've found out. Well, goodness me! It wasn't our fault. It *looked* like a fire. How was anyone to *know*? I bet *they'd* '*ve* thought it was a fire all right. I bet *they'd 've* squirted her, too. . . . Corks! Wasn't she mad! It was a jolly good thing there was all that mist about so's they didn't see us."

"Wouldn't he be mad if he knew!" chuckled Ginger.

"Yes," said Douglas, "but he's not likely to find out now."

But they were wrong. Section Officer Perkins had already found out. Chance had most unkindly delivered the Outlaws into his hand. He was going out to a neighbouring shop for some cigarettes when it happened. He met the small boy who had taken William's message coming out of a sweetshop.

Questioned, he gave a clear and concise account of the circumstances in which he had been sent to summon the A.F.S. to the "fire". He described William and the Outlaws and their fire-fighting equipment in a way that left no room for doubt.

Section Officer Perkins bore down upon the Outlaws just as they were setting out for home. There was a grimly triumphant gleam in his eye. He had made further inquiries since meeting the small boy and had come prepared to give a knock-out blow to his enemies.

They listened with impassive faces and silent dismay to his short but pointed speech. He had discovered, he said, that it was they who had played the "disgraceful trick" on him this morning, sending for him to a fire, when they knew perfectly well that there was no fire at all. He had got all their names and addresses and was going to see the father of each of them that evening. He hoped they would be severely punished. If ever he caught them on that piece of waste ground again he would send for the police. . . . Then he swung on his heel and went away, smiling to himself. The Outlaws stared after him.

"Corks!" said William at last.

"Crumbs!" said Ginger.

"Gosh!" said Douglas and Henry simultaneously.

"My father'll be mad," said Ginger. "He'll never b'lieve we weren't playing a trick on 'em."

"Neither will mine," agreed the other Outlaws gloomily.

"We're goin' to get in an awful row," said William. "'S never any good tellin' my father what really happened. He won't even listen."

"Neither will mine," agreed the other Outlaws.

"I shan't mind not comin' here again," said William. "I was gettin' tired of it, anyway. I'm sick of jus' drillin' an' dustin' the wheelbarrow—I mean the trailer—an' that's all they seem to do. I've jolly well had enough of it, an' I'd 've stopped to-morrow anyway, but—corks! I'm goin' to have an awful time! My father was mad last night 'cause an old woman came tellin' tales about me breakin' her cucumber frame. I was only tryin' to hit a tree with a stone. I didn't *mean* it to go in her old cucumber frame. Gosh! You should've heard the way he went on at me. He said he was sick of people complainin' an' the nex' time it happened he'd give me somethin' to remember an' I bet he jolly well will, too. He's got an awful temper."

Gloomily the Outlaws all agreed that their fathers had awful tempers, too.

"D'you think if we went to him and explained. . . ." said Ginger.

"No, not him!" said William, who was on the whole a fairly good judge of human nature. "He wouldn't b'lieve us, anyway, an' he'd jus' enjoy bein' nasty."

"If we said we were sorry. . . ." said Henry tentatively.

He'd enjoy that still more," said William, "an' he'll

go'n' complain to our fathers jus' the same whatever we do."

"I'd jolly well like to give him somethin' to complain of," said Ginger bitterly.

William looked thoughtful for a few moments, then said slowly:

"Yes . . . that wouldn't be a bad idea. . . . That wouldn't be a bad idea at all. . . . If I've gotter get into a row I'd rather get into it for doin' somethin' worth doin'. My father couldn't be worse than he's goin' to be, anyway, an' I'd like to do somethin' to get even with old Monkey-face."

The Outlaws brightened. Better go down with colours flying. . . . Better strike a blow at the enemy before yielding to superior force.

"What can we do?" said Douglas.

"Well, that's what we've gotter think out," said William.

A new animation possessed the little band. Secretly each had been growing bored with such limited scope as their A.F.S. activities allowed them, and welcomed the wider field afforded by a plan of revenge.

"We've gotter find out somethin' about him first," said William. "Where he lives an' such-like. When I have a revenge I like to take a bit of trouble over it. I'm jolly good at revenges," he ended modestly.

"We'll all have a good think," said Ginger. "Anyway, it's nearly one o'clock now an' we'd better go home. 'S no good getting into any more rows. We've all got a jolly big one comin' to-night, anyway."

"A'right," said William. "We'll meet in the ole barn after lunch. Let's all have a jolly good think while we're havin' lunch. . . . Hope it's jam roly-poly. I can think better on jam roly-poly than on rice puddin'."

They met in the old barn soon after two o'clock. By a

lucky chance Henry's family had been discussing Section
Officer Perkins during lunch and he came primed with
news of him.

"He lives at that house called Green Gates jus'
outside Hadley an' he's not married——"

"'Spect he is, an' murdered her," put in William
darkly.

"An' he's got a housekeeper, but she's had to go
home to look after her father what's ill an' he was askin'
Mrs. Monks if she knew of another an' she said she'd
try 'n' find him one. He's jus' got a char in the mornings
now."

"'Spect he murdered that housekeeper," said William. "He'd 've murdered us soon as look at us."

"Well, what're we goin' to do to him?" said Ginger.

"Have our revenge on him," said William.

"Yes, but how?"

"Well, it wasn't jam roly-poly," said William, "but I
got a sort of idea."

"What was it?" said Douglas.

"Suet pudding 'n' syrup. Better than rice puddin'
anyway."

"No, I meant the idea."

"Oh, yes," said William. "Well, it's gotter be somethin' to do with the A.F.S. Somethin' to do with a hose or
water or somethin'."

"We've not got a hose," said Henry, "an' if we
squirted him with a syringe we'd get in a worse row than
ever."

"I was wond'rin' about the bucket of water," said
William.

"What about it?"

"I was wond'rin' if we could fix it up over a door so's it
fell down soon as he opened it. I've read of people doin'
that. It'd be a jolly good revenge."

The Outlaws considered the idea with interest. There was something of poetic justice in it that appealed to them. Section Officer Perkins had got them into trouble over water. It was only fair that he should get into trouble himself over water. It would be a glorious and fitting end to the Outlaws' branch of the A.F.S. thus thoroughly to douse the man who had brought about its end.

"Might be difficult to fix up," said Douglas dubiously.

"We can try, anyway," said William. "We can have a jolly good try. I bet it won't be difficult."

"Well, he's bein' down at the garage all this afternoon," said Henry. "I found out that. That'll give us time."

"We'll have to be careful," said Douglas.

"Oh, we'll be careful all right," said William carelessly. "Corks! When I think of him goin' into that room an' the bucket of water fallin' right over his head. . . ."

He chuckled. As usual, he saw the scheme in its finished perfection, magnificently ignoring the intervening details.

Again Douglas looked doubtfully at the bucket.

"It's jolly heavy to carry full of water," he said. "I dunno how we're goin' to get it fixed up on top of a door."

"Oh, we'll find a way," said William. "First thing to do is to get it to the house. . . . We'll get it there, an' then we'll find a way to fix it up all right. Come on. . . . 'S time we started."

They filled the bucket with water and carried it in turn across the fields to the outskirts of Hadley. As each one took the weight of the bucket he felt secret doubts about the success of the scheme, but William's glorious optimism swept them along with it.

"We c'n stand on a chair," he said vaguely. "We'll fix

it up all right, once we get it there. I bet it'll be easy fixin' it up, once we get it there."

They approached Green Gates cautiously from the back, making their way into the garden—a neat little garden with an ornamental pond—by way of the hedge and sending Ginger on in front to spy out the land.

"'S empty all right," he said when he returned. "There's no one in it. An' there's a room full of steam same as there was in that cottage this mornin'. He must've left a kettle on, too."

Still carrying the bucket, they approached nearer. William put down the bucket and stared in at a downstairs window through clouds of eddying smoke.

"Gosh! This *is* a fire, all right," he said. "I can see flames. G'n' ring up the fire station, Henry," he went on, "an' I bet we put it out before they come."

He flung up the window and carefully lifted himself and the bucket of water into the room, then flung the water in the direction of the flame. There was a sizzling sound.

"Good!" said William, half choked with smoke. "Get some more water from the pond."

Ginger filled the bucket there and handed it to William through the window. Douglas fought his way into the kitchen and finding another bucket there, filled it at the tap. Gradually the flames died down, leaving a large hole burnt in the carpet, the walls and ceilings blackened.

At that moment the fire brigade arrived. The Outlaws, their faces blackened almost beyond recognition, received them proudly.

"We've put it out," they said.

The captain entered and looked round the water-logged room.

"It wasn't *much* of a fire, of course," said William

modestly, "but it cert'nly was a fire."

"Yes, it certainly was a fire," agreed the captain. His practised eye fell on the groove burnt on the table obviously by a lighted cigarette before it fell on to the carpet.

At that moment the A.F.S. arrived, headed by Section Officer Perkins, looking white and tense. The captain met him at the door.

"Well, Perkins," he said with rather a malicious smile, "you're just too late. So were we, as a matter of fact. . . . You left a lighted cigarette on the table, didn't you?"

"Y-y-yes," stammered Section Officer Perkins. "I—I remembered as soon as the call came through. The telephone went and I put down my cigarette to answer it and then someone came round with a car to give me a lift to the garage and I quite forgot about the cigarette and——"

"Well, you've got these plucky boys to thank for putting it out," said the captain, waving his hand towards the blackened Outlaws.

Section Officer Perkins turned to the blackened Outlaws, recognised them slowly through their coating of grime, and stared at them as though he couldn't believe his eyes. His mouth dropped open. He looked like a man in the throes of a nightmare. He gasped and gulped.

"W-w-w-what happened?" he said at last.

"They saw the fire," said the captain, "and very pluckily came in and put it out. They telephoned us as well. They've shown great pluck and presence of mind, and I think you ought to be very grateful to them."

"Y-y-yes," stammered Section Officer Perkins. "Yes, of course, I am."

"A very dangerous habit, leaving lighted cigarettes

AT THAT MOMENT THE A.F.S ARRIVED, HEADED BY SECTION
OFFICER PERKINS.

about," said the captain. He had always dislike Section
Officer Perkins and was enjoying his discomfiture.

"Y-y-yes," stammered Section Officer Perkins.

He was still staring at the four Outlaws in the manner
of a fascinated rabbit, as if he could never take his eyes
off them again. If he hadn't—unfortunately—remembered putting his cigarette down at the sound of the
telephone bell and not going back into the room again,

"WELL, PERKINS," SAID THE CAPTAIN WITH RATHER A
MALICIOUS SMILE, "YOU'RE JUST TOO LATE."

he would have thought they'd set fire to the place
themselves. They were devils enough for anything.
. . . But the captain of the fire brigade was shaking
hands with them and obviously expecting him to do the
same. He did it, muttering unintelligible thanks and
congratulations. William savoured the moment to the
full, then said carelessly:

"I s'pose you won't be goin' round to see our fathers
to-night?"

"N-n-n-no," stammered Section Officer Perkins.
"No, of course not." He was thoughtfully silent for a
moment, then went on: "Er—how did you come to see

the fire at all? You couldn't have seen it from the road."

But William hadn't thought out the answer to that question yet. He pretended not to hear it.

"Come on," he said to his Outlaws. "Time we went home to tea."

Chapter 5

William Makes a Corner

It seemed to William that the house re-echoed nowadays to the sound of the words "war" and "economy". It was the answer to every complaint, every request.

"Not had a decent bit of Stilton since the war began," grumbled Mr. Brown, and Mrs. Brown replied: "We can't afford Stilton, dear. We have to economise. The grocer's cheese is really quite nice. . . . He recommends it very strongly." "'Strongly' is the word," commented Mr. Brown. And, when Mrs. Brown remarked that she had been wearing her fur coat for three years and she really did not think that it would hang together another winter, Mr. Brown said firmly: "Then you'll have to wear it in pieces, my dear. There's a war on."

And, when William, in his turn, grumbled that sweets had gone up but that his pocket-money remained the same, both turned on him with:

"Don't be ridiculous, William. Sweets indeed! Don't you realise that there's a war on and we all have to economise?"

"But Monster Humbugs a penny each!" he persisted indignantly. "They used to be a halfpenny. They used to last twenty minutes an' they only last quarter of an hour now. A whole *penny* for a *quarter* of an hour. Gosh! It's wicked!"

William and his friends had always been addicted to

Monster Humbugs—enormous striped monstrosities the size of a Victoria plum—and his family had been inclined to encourage the taste as, they said, it ensured comparative silence for at least ten minutes.

Despite his indignation, however, William became interested in the various devices adopted by the household with a view to "war economy". He watched the cook mixing butter and margarine. ("No one'd ever tell the difference," said Cook proudly, whose idea it was. "Wouldn't they?" said the housemaid bitterly. "Well, I would for one.") He watched his mother making a cake with egg substitute. ("It doesn't seem quite honest somehow," sighed Mrs. Brown, "but, after all, it's war time"), and renovating an old sheet by turning it "sides to middle". ("I've read about people doing it, of course, but I never thought I'd ever do it myself. It would have seemed mean in peace time. It's really quite interesting to see how it's done. . . .") He watched Ethel engaged in the uncongenial task of darning a hole in the front of the foot of a silk stocking. ("Just where it shows!" she said passionately. "I'd rather have *died* than be seen with a darn there before the war.") He watched Robert, who had had to give up his motor-cycle but found all other means of transit unsatisfactory, trying with much energy and ingenuity but with little success to fix a home-made motor on to his pedal cycle. Robert's remarks during the process were more interesting and less quotable than those of the rest of the family, and William listened to them happily till in an unguarded moment he ventured to offer advice, whereupon Robert, eyes gleaming wildly from a mask of oil, his person hung about with bits of machinery, turned on him savagely.

"Get out, you, or I'll——"

And William had the sense to get out.

He began to feel that he, too, would like to take part in this war economy campaign. True, he had perforce taken part in it by a curtailment of such pre-war dainties as cream, iced cakes, lumps of sugar and the raised price of Monster Humbugs, but these economies had been, as it were, forced upon him. He wanted to initiate something of his own.

He considered the question at intervals during the day, and that evening approached his mother with the result of his deliberations.

"Mother," he said, "you know Father's always grumblin' about my school bills?"

"Yes, dear," sighed Mrs. Brown. "He says the fees are scandalous."

"Well," said William, "I've been thinkin' about how I can help."

"You mean, work harder, dear?" said Mrs. Brown.

"N-no," said William. "I wasn't thinkin' of that so much. I mean, I do work hard. I'm just wore out with workin' hard sometimes. No, I was thinkin' that if I didn't go to school, he wouldn't have to pay the scand'lous fees. . . . No, listen," he pleaded, as he saw an indignant negative already forming itself on his mother's lips. "I don't want to grow up ign'runt same as you say I will if I don't go to school. I don't want *that*." His tone expressed righteous horror at the idea. "I jolly well don't want to grow up ign'runt, all right. But I can easy learn by myself. I can sort of do sums by myself as I go about. You know. Count and subtract an' such-like. An' I can read stuff out of books. It's all in books. Every bit of it's in books. People what teach, teach out of books, an' it seems to me it's jolly 'stravagant payin' a lot of money for people to teach you out of books when you could learn straight out of books yourself without payin' anythin' but what the books cost."

"No, William," said Mrs. Brown firmly. "You're *certainly* not going to leave school, so you needn't ask again."

"Jus' for the war," pleaded William. "I'll go back at the end of the war. I—I—I'll do war work. I'll help you in the house——"

"*No*, William," said Mrs. Brown with a shudder.

Her tone was so final that William wasted no further words on that particular proposition. He passed on to the next.

"How much money does it cost you to keep me, Mother?" he said. "I mean jus' food."

Mrs. Brown considered.

"Well, really, I don't know exactly, dear," she said. "I should say about fifteen shillings a week."

"Well, tell you what," said William generously. "You give me ten shillin's an' I'll buy my own food. I won't come home to meals at all. That'll save money, all right, won't it? That'll save you five shillin's a week. . . ."

His eyes brightened at the thought of the luscious fare that he could provide for himself on ten shillings a week . . . stacks of doughnuts . . . piles of buns . . . chocolate cakes . . . sherbet . . . lollypops . . . Monster Humbugs. . . . No more rice pudding, or bread and butter or porridge. . . .

"*No*, William," said Mrs. Brown more firmly than ever.

"Seven shillin's then," William tried to tempt her. "I'll buy all the food I want for seven shillin's a week. Think how nice it'll be not havin' me home for meals. Ethel's always sayin' I make her sick watchin' me eat. Well, it'll be nice for Ethel not bein' made feel sick watchin' me eat. An' I bet you'll all like it. You're always goin' on at me, sayin' I've no manners."

"Do stop talking nonsense, William," said Mrs. Brown.

"Seems to me you don't want me to help win the war," said William pathetically. "What about me doin' without clothes?" as another brilliant idea struck him. "You're always sayin' what a lot my clothes cost. I'll do without clothes an' paint myself same as the Anshunt Britons. I've always wanted to try that. I——"

"William!" said Mrs. Brown, "will you *stop* talking nonsense! All we want you to do is to be quiet and good and obedient and——"

But William had gone groaning from the room.

It seemed impossible, however, to escape the subject.

"Soap!" said Mr. Brown bitterly that evening at dinner. "Just plain soap, that's all it is."

"Nonsense, dear!" said Mrs. Brown mildly. "The grocer says it's very good cheese. He says he always has it himself. Of course he admits that it isn't Stilton——"

"Never!" interpolated Mr. Brown.

"——but the housekeeping money simply won't run to Stilton nowadays. Prices are going up all round. One must economise somewhere."

"I've been tryin' to help her 'conomise," said William to Mr. Brown. "I've s'gested lots of things, but she won't listen to 'em."

Mr. Brown, glad of a legitimate object for his irritation, turned on William.

"When you, my boy, make any appreciable contribution to war economy in this household I'll eat my hat."

"All right," said William.

He spoke meaningly, but, in view of the look in his father's eye, discreetly forbore to prolong the discussion.

The more he thought over the remark, however, the more determined he was to take up the challenge. He *would* make a contribution to the economy of the household. His suggestions for saving money on school, food and clothes bills had been treated with contempt, but he would not bear malice on that account. He would do something striking and spectacular. Nothing niggling or cheeseparing for him. No darning of old socks or turning of old sheets or tinkering with old pedal cycles. He'd do the thing in style. He'd be a millionaire. He'd make thousands of pounds. His father should have a Stilton cheese. He himself would have as many Monster Humbugs as he wanted. He had always meant to be a millionaire sooner or later, and there seemed no reason why it shouldn't be sooner. There were hundreds of millionaires. . . . It must be quite easy to be one. "War profiteers. . . ." He had heard his father talking about them only the other day. They were people who made money in war time. He'd be a war profiteer. He'd make money in war time. . . . Having come to that conclusion it only remained for him to decide how to do it. . . . He approached Cook, who, from a wide reading of the Sunday papers, was an accepted authority on most subjects.

"Cook," he said, resting his elbows on the kitchen table and absent-mindedly abstracting a sultana from a small pile on the kitchen table, "how do people get to be war profiteers?"

"You leave them sultanas alone, Master William," said Cook sternly. "I've just weighed 'em out for a pudden."

"Well, I only took one," said William.

"Yes, I know you and your ones," said Cook darkly. "It's one an' one an' one an' one an' one till there's none left. Them sultanas are for a pudden—not for you to go guzzlin' at."

"All right," said William, transferring his attention, but without enthusiasm, to the candied peel. "Can't see why people eat this stuff."

"COOK," SAID WILLIAM, "HOW
DO PEOPLE GET TO BE WAR
PROFITEERS?"
"YOU LEAVE THEM SULTANAS
ALONE, MASTER WILLIAM," SHE
SAID STERNLY.

"Well, you seem to be eatin' it all right." said Cook.

"Well, I've gotter eat *somethin'*," said William. "D'you want me to starve?"

"*Starve!*" said Cook with a sarcastic laugh. "I like that! What about that breakfast you had? Enough for ten, that was."

"That was hours ago," said William, neatly abstracting half a dozen sultanas as Cook turned her back for a second. "Well, nearly an hour ago anyway. . . . Listen, Cook, how do people get to be war profiteers?"

"They—well, they—make money out of a war," explained Cook succinctly.

"But how do they make money?"

They're kings," said Cook, still more succinctly.

"Kings?" said William, deftly abstracting another half-dozen sultanas.

"You know," said Cook. "Wheat kings and match kings and so on."

"Oh," said William slowly, "but how do they *get* to be kings?"

"You leave them sultanas *alone*, Master William," said Cook, "or I won't tell you nothin' more!" Unable, however, to resist the opportunity of airing her knowledge she added: "They make corners."

"Corners?"

"Corners in oil or—or pepper or such-like. Buy up all there is an' charge what they like for it. People've got to pay it 'cause it's all there is. Clever blokes they are," she commented admiringly, then, her sympathy suddenly surging round to their victims, added: "Grindin' the faces of the poor, the devils!"

"I bet it's not hard to make corners," said William. "I bet I could do it!"

"*You!*" said Cook. "You and your corners! . . . Here! Stop cornerin' my sultanas or I'll tell your ma!"

"All right," said William, hastily snatching another handful and making good his escape. "You wait! You *wait*!" he repeated, putting his head in at the kitchen door again and dodging the rolling-pin that Cook made a feint of hurling at him. "You wait till I'm king of something, then you'll wish you'd let me have your rotten ole currants."

He wandered into the garden, munching sultanas and pondering the question of his millionaire career.

. . . Matches. . . . He had a wild idea of collecting used matches, putting fresh heads on and selling them again, but even he realised that the plan was beset with almost insuperable difficulties. Wheat . . . pepper. . . . He didn't see how he could possibly obtain enough supplies of either of these to constitute a "corner". He was still considering the question when the lunch-bell rang and he went indoors. He continued to consider the question while doing full justice to the steak and kidney pie for which Cook was famous. What else were there kings of? Anything, he supposed. Tea, coffee, salt. . . . But Cook was so mean that she'd never let him get enough of any of these commodities to make a proper corner . . . . For no particular reason he began to listen to the grown-up conversation around him.

"I met Jones, the builder, in Hadley this morning," said Robert. "He said that timber was almost unobtainable."

"Timber?" said William.

"Wood, dear," said Mrs. Brown. "It's war, of course."

"Is this supposed to be sultana pudding?" said Ethel bitterly.

"Yes, dear."

"There's hardly a single sultana in it."

"It comes from Sweden, of course," said Robert, "and Sweden's practically cut off."

"I thought they came from Smyrna," said Mrs. Brown. "I'm sure I learnt that in geography when I was a child."

"I'm talking about timber," explained Robert.

"Oh, I see. . . . There ought to be half a pound in it."

"There are exactly two in the piece I've got," said Ethel.

"There's one in mine," said Robert.

"I'll ask Cook about it," said Mrs. Brown.

"Please, mum," said Emma the housemaid, "Cook said if anything was said to say that Master William ate them and bein' war time she didn't like to weigh out any more."

"Me?" said William indignantly. "*Me?* I like that. Well," carrying his mind back with some difficulty to the earlier hours of the day, "perhaps I had one. Well, I may've had *two*, but—well, I think it's nicer without 'em. I think they spoil puddin's. They just take up room where the suet might be, an' suet's better for you than currants in war time."

"That's enough, William," said Mrs. Brown. "I'm always telling you not to meddle with Cook's things. You mustn't have a second helping."

"People've *starved* livin' on as little as this," said William plaintively, looking down at his plate.

"Now, William, that's enough," said Mrs. Brown.

William finished his meal in silence, enduring aloofly the insults of Robert and Ethel, who likened him in turn to most of the less attractive denizens of the zoo. As a matter of fact, he didn't hear them. His mind had gone back to the question of the wood shortage. That surely was something he could make a corner in. Wood. . . . Old Jones had said that it was almost unobtainable. And Coombe Wood was full of it. Twigs, branches, even whole trunks, lay littered about everywhere. There had been some big gales lately and so many of the keepers had been called up that it seemed to be no one's business to clear the paths. That settled it. He'd be a wood king. He'd make a wood corner. . . . The same idea, of course, might occur to anyone else at any moment, so there was no time to lose.

"Can't I really have a second helping, Mother?" he said.

"No, William," said Mrs. Brown.

"Then can I go, please?"

"Yes," said Mrs. Brown.

"Thank heaven!" said Robert.

"What a relief!" said Ethel.

William turned with dignity at the door.

"You wait," he said mysteriously. "You jolly well wait. You'll be sorry one day that you made all this fuss about a few mingy ole currants." And retreated quickly before they could gather breath to reply.

He went to the garden shed and looked about him. He must find some receptacle for his wood corner. He looked speculatively at the gardener's wheelbarrow, but it was a large unwieldy vehicle and had always seemed to have a grudge against him. It would go straight for a few yards then suddenly without warning or reason topple over on to one side. . . . There remained his soap-box on wheels—a smaller but much more manageable affair. It would hold quite a lot of wood, too. Almost a corner, surely. If it didn't hold quite a corner he could go back and fetch more.

He set off in a brisk business-like way to Coombe Wood. Yes, it was everywhere—boughs, branches, twigs, logs. He filled his cart, then made his way towards Hadley. Jones the builder. . . . Pity he didn't know where he lived or anything about him. He ought to have found out from Robert, but Robert had been making such a sickening fuss about a few mingy ole currants that probably he wouldn't have told him even if he'd asked. . . . He slowed his pace as he approached the town. A boy was coming towards him along the road. He looked an earnest and officious sort of boy, the sort of boy who would know everyone else's business as well as his own and be ready and willing to impart his knowledge. William stopped.

"I say," he said, "d'you know where Mr. Jones lives?"

"Yes," said the boy promptly. "Second house from the end down that road. The one with green shutters."

William went down the road to which the boy had pointed. Yes, the second house from the end had green shutters. It must be Mr. Jones's. There was no builder's sign outside, but this must be his private residence. Probably, the builder's yard was down in Hadley. It was in private residences, of course, that kings discussed corners. . . . After hesitating for a few moments, he left his cart in the road and making his way up to the front door, rang the bell. No one came. He rang again. Still no one came. He wandered round to the back door and knocked. A woman opened it. She was a small, thin, worried-looking woman wearing an overall.

"Oh dear!" she greeted him. "I hope you've not been ringing at the front door."

"Yes, I have," said William.

"Oh dear, I'm so sorry," said the woman, looking smaller and thinner and more worried than ever. "It's out of order. I keep meaning to get it mended but I'm so busy with one thing and another just now that I never seem to have time. Have you come for the empties? I'll just see if there are any."

She vanished before William had time to speak and reappeared with a small tonic-water bottle.

"That's all there is," she said apologetically. "Perhaps it's hardly worth your while taking it. . . . Mr. and Mrs. Jones only drink water, and I drink very little——"

"No. I've not come for that," said William. "I've brought a wood corner for Mr. Jones. I've left it round in the front."

"Oh dear, dear!" sighed the little woman. "I'm sick of him and his wood. Mess, mess, mess, all over the place.

Well, I suppose it can't be helped. He's out just now, but you can take it into the front room. That's where he keeps his wood things."

"Y-yes," stammered William, taken aback by the swift conclusion of what should have been a long and complicated business. "But what about payin' for it?"

"Oh, that's all right," said the woman easily. "He'll pay you. Are you in a hurry for the money?"

"Yes," said William simply.

"Well, come round this evening. He's sure to be in then. You can put it in the front room yourself, can't you? I'm too busy to see to it just now. I'm in the middle of one of those frightful war-time cookery recipes of his. They drive me crazy. I'll just open the front door for you. You can manage yourself, can't you?"

With that she disappeared abruptly.

William still stood for a few moments, staring about him in bewilderment, then returned to the road, took his "corner" and made his way round to the front door. The worried-looking woman had evidently opened it in the meantime, but there was no sign of her beyond a "Dear, dear!" from the kitchen, together with the sound of something boiling over.

William left his cart in the hall and opened the door of the front room. Half of it was furnished as a sitting-room, the furniture crowded together anyhow. The carpet was rolled away from the other half, and on the bare floor was a carpenter's bench, some fretwork tools and a crudely executed fretwork bracket.

William glanced about him, interested but puzzled. The thing was not turning out at all as he had meant it to. Surely "kings" didn't just tip their "corners" down in small front rooms like this. . . . Still, he didn't want to take the stuff home again, and the worried looking woman had definitely told him to leave it there and come

WILLIAM BROUGHT THE CART IN AND HAD JUST TIPPED ITS
CARGO OF TWIGS OUT ON TO THE FLOOR, WHEN A SHORT STOUT
MAN APPEARED SUDDENLY IN THE DOORWAY.

back for the money, so it must be all right. At least he
hoped it was all right. He brought the cart in, and had
just tipped its cargo of twigs out on to the floor, when a
short, stout man appeared suddenly in the doorway.
Behind him was a short, stout woman. William knew at

BEHIND HIM WAS A SHORT, STOUT
WOMAN. "WHAT'S THE MEANING OF
THIS," SAID THE MAN. HOW *DARE*
YOU BRING THAT STUFF IN HERE?"

once that he was not going to like them, and that they
were not going to like him. The little man strutted into
the room. He had a round face, a self-important
expression and a small waxed moustache. His face at the
moment was red as well as round, and bad-tempered as
well as self-important.

"What's the meaning of this?" he said. "How *dare* you bring that stuff in here?"

"Yes, how *dare* you?" echoed the woman.

They advanced upon him threateningly, and William took a step backward.

"She—she told me to put it here," he said, pointing in the direction of the kitchen.

"She *told* you?" spluttered the man. His face deepened from red to purple and the pointed ends of his moustache quivered with rage. "I don't believe you."

"Not a word, I don't," said the woman.

"She did. Honest she did," said William. "You see it's a corner an'——"

"Get out," said the man.

"This very moment, get out," said the woman.

They were close upon him—large and angry and overpowering. It was not, William felt, a propitious moment for delicate financial negotiations. He darted between them, out of the open front door, and fled homewards.

Miss Jones hung anxiously over the baked orange soufflé recipe that her cousin had ordered as a sweet for dinner. She disliked cooking, and when she lived alone had lived quite happily on such snacks as kippers, boiled ham, sausages and beans on toast—things that either didn't need cooking or, so to speak, cooked themselves. When her cousin wrote, asking her to take him and his wife as paying guests for the period of the war, she had agreed without enthusiasm, but from a sense of family duty.

Mr. and Mrs. Jones were professional bomb-dodgers. They had left London for Scotland at the outbreak of war. They had left Scotland for the south coast after the first Scottish raid. They had left the south coast for Cornwall after the fall of Belgium, and Cornwall for

Wales after the fall of France. And now, after the first raid in their neighbourhood in Wales, they had written to Miss Jones asking her to take them in. After each move they had left behind them a household of shattered and exhausted friends or relations, on whom they had parked themselves and who generally considered the raid that had finally relieved them of their guests not too high a price to pay.

"Poor things!" Miss Jones had said when she received their letter. "They won't be much trouble. And they'll be so grateful."

She had since revised her opinion. They were quite a lot of trouble, and they were not at all grateful. Mr. Jones, whose hobby was the making of unnecessary articles of indescribably hideous design in fretwork, insisted on using her best sitting-room as a workshop, because he said that the shed she had provided for the purpose was draughty. His culinary requirements were varied and complicated. He didn't like any of the things that Miss Jones could cook, and he had bought a book of "war cookery recipes" that appeared to differ from peace-time recipes in being twice as much trouble. He grumbled incessantly. He grumbled at the beds, he grumbled at the food and he grumbled at the house; he strewed the place with bits of fretwork; he had ruined her sitting-room; and he didn't pay enough to cover his keep. . . . Miss Jones had several times tried to screw up courage to ask him to go, but always it failed her at the last moment. For Miss Jones was a timid soul and easily frightened, and Mr. Jones, when his moustache bristled and his round face went purple, scared the life out of her. Mrs. Jones was no better. She expected to be waited on hand and foot, and she echoed all her husband's complaints with an offensiveness that was peculiarly her own.

Miss Jones had been on the verge of tears when William arrived with his "corner". The baked orange soufflé that Mr. Jones had demanded for his dinner was, as she said, "frightful". You had to put grated orange rind into milk and boil it, then infuse (and Miss Jones was not at all sure what "infuse" meant) and strain and boil again. Then you had to melt margarine in a saucepan and stir in flour and "beat well". Miss Jones had only just begun it and already she was in a hopeless muddle. The fact that she herself couldn't eat anything with orange in added bitterness to the situation.

"Drat the man!" she said as she measured out milk and margarine. "*Drat* the man!" but she knew that if he asked her to make it again to-morrow she wouldn't dare refuse. . . .

And then—just after the milk was boiling over for the second time—a boy arrived bringing some fretwork nonsense or other (a "wood corner" he called it) for Mr. Jones. It seemed the last straw and it was all she could do to keep her temper. It wasn't only Mr. Jones's fretwork nonsense that irritated her. It was the airs he put on about it. He seemed to consider himself the world's greatest fretwork artist. Still—it wasn't the boy's fault, so Miss Jones just sent him round to the front door with it and returned to the soufflé. Then— as she was mopping up the milk that had boiled over—came the sound of the entry of the Joneses followed by the sound of voices. Mr. Jones's voice, the boy's voice . . . Mr. Jones's voice upraised in anger. . . . Wrong sort of corner, she supposed. The *fuss* the man made! Mr. Jones entered the kitchen, his moustache bristling, his face purple.

"Did you tell that boy to put that stuff in the front room?" he demanded.

"Yes," said Miss Jones, her spirits sinking. (Oh dear, she'd done the wrong thing, evidently.) "I did."

"An insult!" shouted Mr. Jones. "A deliberate insult! I've put up with a lot, but deliberate insults to my art I will *not* put up with. I leave the house to-day."

"Oh," said Miss Jones, her spirits rising again.

"Yes, to-day," repeated Mr. Jones. "I will not stay a second longer in a place where my art is ridiculed and deliberate insults are heaped upon it."

"I didn't really know it was the wrong sort of corner," Miss Jones justified herself mildly.

"Don't argue with me," shouted Mr. Jones. "In any case you let me come here under false pretences. You had two air-raid warnings only last week."

"They were quite little ones," Miss Jones excused herself.

Mr. Jones cut short her excuses.

"Don't talk nonsense," he said. "The thing was a calculated and deliberate insult. . . . I'm going up to pack this moment." He turned to his wife. "We'll try Cheshire, my dear. That should be fairly safe. And your aunt's cousin lives there, doesn't she?"

Miss Jones sat down heavily on a kitchen chair.

Mrs. Jones threw her a final "Outrageous!" and went out slamming the door.

Miss Jones got up from the kitchen chair, drew a deep breath, removed the unfinished orange soufflé, brought a kipper out of her larder and slipped it into the oven for her supper.

* * *

It was dark when William arrived at the back door. Miss Jones answered his knock.

Her small thin face wore a look of shining happiness. The Joneses had departed, the shouting and the tumult had died, and peace had descended once more upon the little house. The kipper had been excellent. She'd enjoyed it more than she ever remembered enjoying a kipper in all her life.

"Is he in?" said William, looking round the kitchen.

"They're gone," said Miss Jones. "Packed up and gone in less than an hour. Gone to Cheshire."

William's face fell.

"Gosh! What about my wood corner?"

"That was the trouble," said Miss Jones. "I thought you meant something for his fretwork. A corner, you know. A sort of bracket. . . ."

William gaped at her.

"Didn't you know about corners an' kings an' things?"

"Corners and kings?" said Miss Jones mystified.

William sighed.

"I was tryin' to be a millionaire. I thought he'd pay me for them. I thought he was a builder."

"Oh, no," said Miss Jones, "he's not a builder. There *is* a builder called Jones in Hadley, but he's no relation."

"Gosh!" said William, after a moment's silence. "I'm always makin' a mess of things."

"Well," said Miss Jones, "it's turned out all right for me. I wanted him to go."

"Yes," said William, remembering the small bristling moustache, purple face, and harsh grating voice. "Yes, I bet you did."

"I've wanted him to go for a long time, but I daren't tell him to."

"No," agreed William, remembering them again. "No, I bet you daren't."

"They didn't like anything I liked," continued Miss Jones. "Wouldn't touch kippers or sausages or liver and bacon or anything like that. Wanted things out of books I couldn't make head or tail of. And cheese. There's a whole Stilton in the larder that he hadn't touched. I don't know what to do with it. It's poison to me. . . ."

"I bet my father'd like it, all right," said William.

"Would he?" said Miss Jones. "I wish you'd take it to him then. The smell's turning me sick."

"Can I really take it to him?" said William eagerly. "It'd put him in a good temper, an' it's a long time since he's been in one. He says the grocer's tastes of soap."

"Do take it. I never want to see it again. It reminds me of my cousin, and I want to forget him as quickly as I can. Please ask your father to accept it from me with my compliments."

"Yes, I'll do that, all right," said William. "Thanks awfully."

He thought of his "corner" of wood. There didn't seem much point in going on with the business. If Mr. Jones, the fretwork artist, took his corner as an insult, probably Mr. Jones the builder would do the same.

"That wood . . . ." he said tentatively.

"It would do for laying fires," said Miss Jones, "though, of course, it's a bit small."

"It wouldn't be any good for building then?" said William.

"Building?" said Miss Jones, in surprise. "Oh dear, no."

"No," sighed William, relinquishing his cherished dream, "I suppose not. . . . Would you like it for layin' fires? In exchage for the cheese, sort of?"

"Thanks," said Miss Jones, "I'd like it very much. I was a bit hard up for firewood."

*   *   *

Mr. Brown was in the morning-room when William arrived home.

"I've brought you a Stilton cheese, Father," said William pleasantly.

"Good heavens!" said Mr. Brown. "Where have you stolen it from?"

"A lady gave it me," explained William. "At least she said would I give it to you with her compliments. A lady called Miss Jones, but you don't know her."

Mr. Brown considered the story in silence for some moments, then said:

"Why should a lady I don't know send me a Stilton cheese?"

William looked back over his afternoon and saw it in the bleak hard light of reality.

"I took her a bit of firewood," he explained.

"But I still don't see why she should send me a Stilton cheese," persisted Mr. Brown.

"Well," explained William further, "she had a cousin stayin' with her an' this cousin got mad 'cause of this firewood I gave her an' went off to Cheshire an' she gave me the Stilton cheese for you 'cause it's poison to her an' was turnin' her sick."

Mr. Brown considered this fuller account with increasing mystification. Then he decided that it was, after all, none of his business. William had arrived with a Stilton cheese that had, for all he knew to the contrary, been lawfully acquired. His not to reason why. . . .

"Thank you, my boy," he said. "Very kind of you. Your gift will lighten the horrors of war for me—for the time being at any rate. Soap, the other was, whatever they say. Just soap."

William looked at him speculatively.

"Have I 'tributed to the war economy of the household?" he asked.

"Decidedly," said Mr. Brown. "Most decidedly. It looks a really excellent Stilton."

"You said you'd eat your hat if I did," William reminded him.

"I used that expression, my boy," said Mr. Brown, "in a purely figurative sense."

William thought for a few minutes. He'd had a busy and tiring day and didn't seem to be getting anything out of it.

"I told you that Monster Humbugs were a penny each, didn't I?" he asked.

"I have heard you mention it," said Mr. Brown, "more than once, I believe."

"Well," said William, "I 'spose there's no lor about the name of a sweet? I mean, you can call it what you like, can't you? I mean, if someone called it one thing, someone else could call it another, couldn't they?"

"Undoubtedly," said Mr. Brown, still examining his windfall. "Best Stilton I've seen since the war. The real thing."

"Well, listen," said William. "'spose you gave me sixpence an' I went an' bought six of 'em, an' then brought 'em home an' changed their name from Monster Humbugs to My Hats. Then I'd give one to you an' you'd eat it an' you'd 've kep' your promise an' eaten your hat."

Mr. Brown considered this suggestion, and his rare smile flickered for a second over his grim countenance.

"There's something in it," he said. "Though a receiver of dubiously acquired Stilton, I should, at least, be a man of my word." He put his hand in his pocket and drew out a shilling. "There you are, my boy. And you can keep the change. . . ."

*　　*　　*

William ambled slowly and contentedly along the road. First one cheek bulged, then the other. There was a tense strained look in his eyes that was nevertheless one of rapture. His whole face was distorted as his parted lips appeared to do their utmost to meet over some writhing obstacle that separated them. To a passing stranger he would have appeared to be in the last throes of some unendurable agony, but there were no passing strangers about and his acquaintances would have known that he was merely wrestling with the first few moments of a Monster Humbug, and would have expected no further answer to their greeting than a guttural snort. He had reduced it to a comparatively manageable size by the time he reached the old barn where the other Outlaws awaited him.

"LookatwotI'vegot," he said indistinctly, dragging the bag of Monster Humbugs from his pocket.

They gazed at it incredulously, almost reverently. "*Gosh!*" they said, examining it. "Ten of 'em. *Crumbs!* How did you get 'em?"

William wrestled with speech for some moments and finally removed the Monster Humbug (now about the size of a greengage) from his mouth in order to make his meaning and elocution clearer. Holding the precious morsel carefully between finger and thumb, he gulped, swallowed, and began his explanation.

"Well, I sort of thought I'd make a corner, so I tried wood an' that wasn't any use then I tried humbugs an' I've jolly well made a corner in 'em. It was all because of a Stilton cheese that——"

But the Outlaws were not interested in the story. They were already engaged in complicated mathematical problems, for the Outlaws were communists in the best sense of the word.

"I've had one of mine, an' given my father one," said William, "so the rest of you can have three each." With that he popped the half-sucked dainty back into his mouth.

They crowded round him, holding out grubby palms for their share.

They walked on together down the road, faces distorted, mouths working furiously, cheeks bulging.

A blissful silence reigned. . . .

Chapter 6

The Outlaws and the Parachutist

"Get out of here, you kids!" said the Home Guard man impatiently.

William and the Outlaws withdrew a few steps and continued to watch the fascinating spectacle—Home Guard men with tin hats and uniforms, carrying rifles and manning a fortress of camouflaged sandbags with loopholes for shooting through. It was incredibly impressive, exciting and romantic. . . .

"I said, get on *out* of here," repeated the Home Guard man, advancing threateningly upon them.

The Outlaws knew, of course, that he was only Billy Foxton, the blacksmith, who had let them watch him shoe horses and even occasionally lend a hand, but the tin hat, uniform and rifle invested him with such majesty that, obeying reluctantly, they turned and wandered disconsolately down the road.

"Gosh! I wish I was grown-up," said William. "They have all the fun."

"An' I bet you anythin' the war'll be over by the time we're grown up," said Ginger. "I bet you *anythin'* it will. I bet that when we're grown up we'll jus' have to go to offices with no fun at all. Grown-ups didn't have any fun till this war started, an' they won't have any more when it's over."

"Fancy Billy Foxton with a uniform an' a gun an' a tin hat."

"They've got wire things they can put right across the road, too."

"I know. . . . Tank traps," said Henry.

"Crumbs! Wun't you like to shoot through one of those little holes?"

"One of 'em brought down a German plane the other day."

"Our cook's cousin's a 'contamination man. He wears things jus' like a diver."

"I'd sooner be a Home Guard man. I'd like to shoot through the little holes."

"Our gardener knows a man what's got a friend what knows someone what caught a parachutist dressed up as a woman."

"Gosh!"

"They do that, you know. They dress up as women."

"Crumbs!"

"Yes, if ever you see a woman what looks like a man you c'n be jolly sure it's a parachutist. If we were one of *them* we'd jus' put that wire thing across the road an' start shootin' at 'em through the little holes. Jus' think! They might find one any minute any day. Or whole armies of 'em. An' all we've gotter do"— in a tone of bitter disgust—"is jus' do nothin'. It's not fair."

"An' I bet we could do it all as well as them," said Ginger.

"I jolly well bet we'd do it better."

"An' I don't see why we shouldn't."

"They wouldn't let us."

"Don't see how they could stop us. We'd have one of our own. Somewhere where they've not got one. I bet there's lots of places where they've not got one. An' I bet if we did we'd catch a parachutist before they did."

"It wasn't much good when we had an Auxilliary Fire Service," said Douglas.

"No, but we had it too near the other one," explained William. "They got jealous an' there was that mess-up about that fire. . . . I say, we could get a thing to put across the road, an' we could make a fort with holes in."

"They'd find out we'd got one an' stop us," said Henry again.

"Bet they wouldn't," said William, the optimist. "We'd go somewhere where they couldn't see us. Gosh! There's *hundreds* of roads an' lanes an' places where they haven't got 'em, an' where those ole parachutists might easily come along. . . . Well, I think it's our *juty* to have one."

They considered this aspect of the question in silence. William was, as ever, persuasive, convincing his hearers even against their will.

"We've got no guns," said Douglas at last.

"Well, we've got weapons, haven't we?" said William. "*Weapons* is all you need. We've got an airgun haven't we, an' a pea-shooter, an' catapults, an' bows an' arrows, haven't we? Gosh! I nearly killed our gard'ner with a pea-shooter. At least he told my father I did, an' my father nearly killed me for it. An' I bet I can't count the windows an' things I've broke with my bow an' arrows an' catapult. If they'd all been Germans I bet the war'd 've been over by now."

"We haven't got little holes to shoot through," said Henry.

"We can make 'em, can't we?" said William. "Anyone can make holes, can't they? Well, holes are *there* ready. You've only got to put somethin' round 'em."

"Where'll we have it?" said Ginger.

"Somewhere where they can't see us," said William. "They'll only start bein' jealous an' try to stop us if they see us. They jus' won't *b'lieve* that we can do it as well as what they can. Grown-ups never do. . . ." He paused a moment and considered. "There's that lane that goes from Hadley Road to Marleigh. They've got nothin' there, an' I bet the Germans could use it as a short cut to get to Hadley. They've not thought of that—those ole Home Guard men. They've put forts an' traps an' things all on the main road an' forgot that that lane's a short cut."

"It's too small for tanks to go along," objected Henry.

"Yes, but parachutists dressed up as women could go along it," said William earnestly, "an' I bet they *will*, too, if we don't make a fort there. I bet we've gotter do it jolly *quick*, too. . . . They might be comin' to-night for all we know."

"There's those ole packing-cases in the ole barn," said Ginger thoughtfully. "We could use them."

"An' we've got some ole sandbags," added Douglas. "They took 'em away from in front of our shelter an' built a sort of wall instead."

"An' we've got lots an' lots of wooden seed-boxes in our shed," said Henry. "I bet we could fill 'em up with earth an' they'd do as well as sandbags. . . . I bet our gardener won't notice they've gone."

"An' there's some green paint in our garage," said Ginger. "That'll do for camouflage."

"*Gosh!*" breathed William ecstatically. "We're going to have a *jolly* fine one."

* * *

It took the Outlaws all day to erect the "fort" to their satisfaction. As it happened, no one passed by except a butcher's boy, who was so deeply interested in the proceedings that the butcher was receiving complaints all afternoon of joints delivered too late for lunch, and a village ancient, who was, apparently, so absorbed in memories of the past that he did not even notice it. By

dusk it was completed. It was a somewhat fantastic
construction, taking up, in fact, most of the roadway. At
the base were the seed-boxes from Henry's toolshed
filled with earth and piled on top of each other. Above
these came the sandbags laboriously carried from
Douglas's air-raid shelter, and arranged so as to leave at
intervals gaps forming the "shooting holes", which were
the crowning glory of the whole thing. Above this were
ranged packing-cases brought from loft or boxroom as
well as the old barn. The whole looked so crazy that you
would have thought it would come down at a breath, but
by some miracle of balance it resisted the force of
gravity. Four large stones "borrowed" from Ethel's
rockery were placed at intervals across the remainder of
the road to form a "tank trap". As William pointed out
there was no reason why a parachutist should not land
with a small portable tank along with his motor-bicycle
and other equipment. Finally, the Outlaws took up their
positions in the rear of the fort pointing arrows, air-gun,
pea-shooter and catapult through the "shooting holes".

The minutes passed. The lane remained deserted.
Dusk began to fall.

"We've jus' not gotter mind nothin' happ'nin' at
first," William encouraged his band. "*They've* been
waitin' for months an' months. . . . We've jus' not
gotter mind waitin' months an' months, but it *might*
happen any minute. Any minute we might see a man
dressed up like a woman comin' down the lane an' when
you see a man dressed up like a woman you jolly well
know he's a German parachutist. You——"

"Someone's comin' down now," Ginger whispered
excitedly. "*Gosh!* It looks someone peculiar, too. Bet
you anythin' it's a parachutist."

The figure approached. It was a large, unwieldy
figure. It wore a curious feather-trimmed bonnet tied

under its chin, a rusty black cape, and long, voluminous black skirts. The face beneath the bonnet showed masculine and heavy-featured through the dusk. Stout boots, suggestive of a farm labourer's, appeared beneath the rusty skirts.

"It *is* one of 'em," whispered William tensely. "It's—one, two, three—*fire!*"

"IT *IS* ONE OF 'EM," WHISPERED WILLIAM TENSELY. "IT'S—ONE, TWO, THREE—*FIRE*!"

Air-gun, arrows, peashooter and catapult discharged themselves from behind the "fort" with such devastating effect that the whole ramshackle structure quivered and collapsed, hurling seed-boxes, sandbags, packing cases and Outlaws in glorious confusion to the ground. Having extricated themselves with some difficulty, they retrieved their weapons and looked round for the parachutist. The parachutist lay outstretched and motionless in the middle of the road. In falling beneath the barrage of seed-boxes, sandbags, packing cases and human boys, he had hit his head against one of the rockery stones that formed the "tank trap" and was apparently, for the time being at any rate, knocked out. It was certainly a case of "he". Bonnet and wig had rolled off, revealing a cropped head surmounting an unmistakable male countenance, and the large hands and boots removed all possible further doubt.

"Gosh!" breathed William. "It *is* one!"

"Is he dead?" said Ginger apprehensively. "We'll get in an awful row if he's dead."

William approached the prostrate figure and examined it cautiously.

"No, it's all right," he said. "He's still breathing. He must've fainted or somethin'."

"Hadn't we better go 'n' fetch someone quick?" said Douglas nervously. "He might come to, any minute, an' he looks jolly strong."

"I wonder what's in his bag," said William, picking up the old-fashioned reticule that lay in the road beside the parachutist.

He opened it and drew out a paper. The Outlaws crowded round.

"*Gosh!*" said William. "It's a pass into Marleigh Aerodrome. *Gosh!* He's one of 'em, all right. He came over in a parachute dressed up as a woman with a forged pass into Marleigh Aerodrome."

He examined the paper intently in the fading light. "Yes, it's forged, all right," he pronounced at last. "It's jolly well forged, too. Gosh! We only jus' got him in time. He'd 've blown up the whole place by now."

They stood looking down uncertainly at their unconscious captive.

"What'll we do with him?" demanded Ginger.

"We've gotter get him to the police," said William.

"How?" demanded Douglas. "He'd be jolly heavy to carry an' he's goin' to be mad when he comes to. He'll prob'ly kill us all an' then go off to Marleigh Aerodrome an' blow it up, same as he'd meant to when we stopped him."

"Tell you what we'll do," said William. He turned to Douglas and Henry. "You go an' fetch the police, an' Ginger and me'll guard him."

"All right," said Douglas, obviously relieved to be dismissed. "All right. We'll be as quick as we can. Tell you what. We'll fetch Major Winton. His house is the nearest an' he's a Special Constable. Come on, Henry."

Douglas and Henry vanished into the dusk.

William and Ginger stood guard over the prisoner. William held the bow and arrow, Ginger the air-gun. They looked down somewhat apprehensively at the motionless form. Though motionless, it was massive and muscular.

"I dunno that this bow 'n' arrow's goin' to be much good," said William. "He's too near to take aim prop'ly."

"Same with the air-gun," said Ginger. "He'd jump up and be on us before we'd took aim at him."

"A stick's what we want," said William reflectively. "A good strong stick. Then, when he starts gettin' up we'll jus' hit him on the head with it, an' stun him again till the p'lice come." He glanced across the field at the dim outline of the woods. "It wouldn't take us a minute to go 'n' get one. We'd be back before he's come unstunned."

"All right," agreed Ginger. "Come on."

They ran across the field into the wood and began to

look round for a stout stick. It took longer than they had expected to find one.

"This'll do," said William breathlessly at last, seizing upon a stout piece of ash about the size of a walking stick. "Come on. Let's go back, quick. . . . If he's started comin' unstunned an' the police aren't there yet, I'll give him a good hit with it. . . ."

They hurried back to the road.

The fallen fortress was still there.

The "tank trap" was still there.

But the captured parachutist had vanished. . . .

They stared down incredulously at the spot where they had left him.

"Gosh!" said William at last faintly, and Ginger echoed "*Gosh!*"

"He's gone," said William. "He's come to an' gone. He's probably blown up Marleigh Aerodrome by now."

"He's not got his forged pass," Ginger reminded him. "He can't get in without his forged pass."

"He'll get in somehow," said William. "They're jolly clever, are parachutists. They train 'em special to be clever. He'll probably pretend to be a pilot's mother or somethin'."

"Let's have a good look for him first," said Ginger, "case he's hidin' somewhere round. Keep the stick ready case he jumps out at us."

But an exhaustive search of the lane with its bordering fields and hedges failed to produce any trace of the missing parachutist.

"I bet no one'll believe we found him," said Ginger dejectedly.

"Course they will," said William. "We've got his forged pass, haven't we?"

"Well, I bet he's waitin' somewhere round to spring

out on us an' get his pass back," said Ginger. "Tell you what. I think we oughter take his pass to the police station 'stead of hangin' about with it like this. It's all the proof we've got now he's gone."

"All right," said William. "You take it along to the police station, an' I'll stay here till Douglas and Henry come. They oughter be here any minute."

Ginger vanished into the dusk in the direction of the village and William continued a desultory search of the hedges.

Suddenly voices warned him of the approach of Douglas and Henry, and Major Winton. Major Winton, roused from a comfortable doze in his favourite arm-chair, had listened to their story, first with bewilderment then with incredulity. Finally, so convinced and convincing were the two Outlaws, he had begun to think that there might be something in it. After all, such things had happened in other countries and, impossible as it still seemed, might happen in this.

He stood in the roadway and looked about him—bewildered and still slightly fretful, as a man has a right to be who has been recently roused from a fireside doze. He was tall and thin, had long drooping moustaches and bore a striking resemblance to the White Knight in *Alice Through the Looking Glass*.

He stood in the road and looked about him.

"Well, where is he, where is he?" he said irritably. "And what's all this frightful mess?"

"He's gone," said William, "and that's our fort."

Major Winton looked at him suspiciously.

"If you boys have been playing a trick on me," he began.

"Honest, we haven't" William assured him. "He was a parachutist dressed up as a woman and he'd got a forged pass into Marleigh Aerodrome."

"Well, where is he?" said the major testily, "and where's the pass?"

"We don't know about him," said William. "He got away. But we've got his pass all right. Ginger's jus' taken it to the the p'lice station."

At that moment a policeman appeared. He was a large, stout, official-looking policeman.

"Now then!" he said. "What's all this 'ere?"

The major hailed his appearance with relief.

"These boys say they found a parachutist with a pass into Marleigh Aerodrome," he said.

"Good!" said the policeman. "He's the man we've been looking for, then. Someone's just rung up the station to say that he was attacked and his pass stolen from him."

"Who attacked him?" asked Major Winton with interest.

"He doesn't know. He was knocked out at once, and when he recovered found that the pass was gone. Presumably it was the parachutist these kids say they found." He turned to William. "How d'you know he was a parachutist?"

"He was dressed like a woman," explained William.

"Which way did he go?"

"I dunno," said William. "He ran away while we were getting a stick."

"Where's the pass?"

"Ginger's got it. He's taking it to the police station."

The policeman assumed an air of official dignity.

"I'll go and ask the Home Guard men if they've seen any suspicious-looking characters on the road," he said. "You kids stay here. We may want you again."

And at that moment the parachutist suddenly arrived holding Ginger by the neck. He strode along, his rusty skirts billowing about his stout boots. His face looked set and stern. In his free hand he carried his bonnet and wig.

"*That's* him!" cried William excitedly. "Catch him quick before he gets away."

"I've got the wretch," the parachutist was saying to the policeman. "It was this little villain who pinched my pass, though how he managed to knock me out beats me."

The policeman blinked and stared and finally, forgetting his official dignity, murmured "Blimey!"

Then to be on the safe side he put one hand on the parachutist's shoulder and the other on Ginger's.

"Here!" said the parachutist indignantly, as he shook it off. "I've got to be at the aerodrome by seven-thirty. I've given this boy into custody and I can't waste any more time."

"I like that," burst out William indignantly. "It's us givin' *you* into custody. *You're* the parachutist with a forged pass dressed up as a woman an' *we've* caught you."

"The—*what*?" said the man.

"If you aren't a parachutist," said William triumphantly, "why are you dressed up as a woman with a forged pass?"

"Now then, now then, now then!" said the policeman, taking out his note-book. "Let's get this straight. . . ."

"I'm dressed up as a woman," said the parachutist to William, "because I'm going to give a performance at Marleigh Aerodrome and I have to be back at the Grand Theatre, Hadley, in time for the eight-thirty performance there, so I've no time to change afterwards. I'd no time to change before, because I've been rehearsing at the Grand Theatre, Hadley, up to about half an hour ago. I thought I might risk driving there and back in costume but unfortunately my car broke down on the way, and I was taking a short cut down the lane to the

"*THAT'S* HIM!" CRIED WILLIAM EXCITEDLY.
"CATCH HIM QUICK BEFORE HE GETS AWAY!"

garage on the main road to get help. And my pass is *not* forged. It was issued to me by the commanding officer of the camp in my capacity of guest artist at the variety show they're giving there this evening. They put my 'turn' early so that I could get back in time for my 'turn' at Hadley, but I'm going to be late, I'm afraid. Anything else you'd like to know?"

"Then you aren't a German parachutist dressed up as a woman?" said William.

"Certainly not," said the parachutist indignantly. "Whatever made you think I was?"

"Corks!" said William, with a deep sigh. "We never have any luck."

"You an' your parachutists!" said the policeman shutting his notebook with a snap. "An' a nice mess you've made of the road," he added severely.

"That was our fort," said Ginger mournfully.

"Well, I can't waste any more time here," said Major Winton. "Good night, sir," to the parachutist. "Good night, Constable. And I hope that you boys won't make nuisances of yourselves like this again."

He went home to finish his nap, feeling half relieved and half disappointed that the affair had petered out so tamely.

"I'll be goin', too," said the policeman. "Can't hang about here all night. Thank you, sir," as the parachutist slipped something into his hand. "Glad that it's all been settled satisfactorily. And, you kids," to the Outlaws, "be a bit more careful next time or you'll be getting into trouble."

He went off, leaving parachutist and Outlaws alone.

"Well, we *thought* you were one," said William in a small voice.

The parachutist looked down at the four dejected faces.

"I say," he said suddenly, "how would you like to come to the aerodrome with me and see the show?"

The four dejected faces beamed, sparkled, radiated.

"*Oh!*" gasped William. "*Could* we?"

"I think so," said the parachutist. "I think I can manage it. There's the question of your parents, of course. . . . Suppose you come with me to the garage now and I'll ring them up from there and ask permission. . . ."

*　　*　　*

The Outlaws sat in a crowded hall surrounded by a god-like company of men in Air Force blue—men who sailed the skies and brought down German bombers as regularly and unconcernedly as you and I have marmalade for breakfast.

That in itself would have provided one of the greatest thrills of the Outlaws' lives. But, added to this, the god-like beings were jovial and friendly. They teased Ginger about the colour of his hair. They called William "Old Bill". They gave them humbugs and pear drops.

The parachutist was beginning his repertoire of comic songs from the stage, a repertoire abounding in the immemorial jokes of the music hall.

As a comedian the parachutist had a way with him.

The audience rocked and roared helplessly.

The Outlaws rocked and roared with the best.

William choked till the tears ran down his face.

Ginger's yell of laughter at each fresh sally was like a gun explosion.

Douglas waved and stamped to swell the applause.

Henry was so purple in the face that, had anyone noticed him (which no one did), they would have diagnosed the last stages of an apoplectic fit.

It was the happiest day of their lives.

Chapter 7

William—The Salvage Collector

"Come on, William," called Mrs. Brown. "The siren!"

William stumbled sleepily out of bed, hunched into his dressing-gown, put on his bedroom slippers, collected various bits of cardboard that he was using for his "invention" of an entirely new type of aeroplane, and made his way to the air-raid shelter at the bottom of the garden. Already assembled were Ethel, wearing a siren suit of pale grey corduroy, Emma the housemaid, in a red flannel dressing-gown, her hair in curling papers, her face grim and set, her teeth clasped firmly on an enormous cork, and Mr. Brown, looking sleepy and dishevelled but preparing to re-read his evening paper with an air of philosophical detachment.

Robert was on night duty at the warden's post, and Cook had joined the Forces last week.

Ethel groaned as William entered.

"Oh, gosh!" she said. "I hoped he'd have slept through it."

"Of course not," said Mrs. Brown placidly. "I shouldn't dream of letting him sleep through it. Now, make room for him, dear, and don't be disagreeable."

"Can't I have the hammock?" pleaded William.

Originally a hammock had been slung up for William's use, but the acrobatics in which he had indulged had precipitated him so frequently upon the heads of his family below that, much to his disgust, it had been taken down.

"No, dear," said Mrs. Brown. "You only fidget and fall on people."

"What can I do, then?" demanded William.

"Go to sleep," said Mrs. Brown. "It's long past your bed-time."

"*Sleep?*" echoed William in disgust. "I jolly well wouldn't waste an air raid *sleepin'* in it."

"Well, you must be quiet."

"All right," said William. "I'll go on with my aeroplane. I bet it'll make 'em all sit up when I've finished it. It's a troop-carryin' aeroplane, an' it's goin' to go six hundred miles an hour an' it's goin' to be camouflaged so's to look like a cloud in the sky an' like a barn when it comes down so's the troops can hide in it."

He stopped and listened for a few moments. "That's a Dornier," he pronounced with an air of finality.

"On the contrary, it's a cow," said Mr. Brown, without looking up from his paper.

"Oh, yes, so it is," agreed William as he recognised the note. "It's Farmer Smith's Daisy. She's been carryin' on like that all day."

Mrs. Brown was checking her equipment of spirit kettle, biscuit tins, tea, coffee, milk, fruit and chocolate. She delighted in feeding her family during an air raid, but usually only William appreciated her efforts.

"Anyone like anything to eat or drink?" she asked hopefully.

"Yes, please," said William promptly.

She gave him a glass of lemonade and a couple of biscuits.

"Wouldn't anyone else like something?" she asked. "Tea or coffee or something?"

"Good heavens, Mother!" said Ethel, "we can't go on eating all night."

Mr. Brown glanced at his watch.

"We've only just had dinner, my dear," he said. "The process of digestion can hardly be completed yet."

Emma, appealed to next, shook her head grimly and pointed to her cork. Regretfully Mrs. Brown put her equipment away.

Ethel had taken a small mirror from her bag and was patting her head of red-gold curls.

"Thank heaven I had a perm last week," she said. "I simply couldn't have gone through another raid if I hadn't."

"I don't quite see how you could have avoided it," said Mr. Brown, turning over a sheet of his evening paper.

"I do hope Robert's all right," sighed Mrs. Brown.

"Why shouldn't he be?" said Mr. Brown. "He couldn't very well have got anything more than a chill up to the present."

"Yes, dear," said Mrs. Brown reproachfully, "but, after all, it *is* a raid."

Mr. Brown gave an unfeeling grunt and turned over another sheet of his newspaper.

"Industrials seem to be keeping up pretty well," he commented.

"*That's* a Dornier," said William suddenly. "Right over us, too," he added in a tone of deep satisfaction.

"That is a motor-cycle on the main road," put in Mr. Brown quietly, without looking up from his paper.

"Oh, yes . . . well, they do sound jolly alike."

"Have you ever heard a Dornier?" asked his father.

"Well, I don't know. I may've done. . . . This aeroplane's goin' to have six engines. . . . Can I have somethin' else to eat, Mother? I'm jolly hungry."

"There's the biscuit tin."

"Can't I have some chocolate?"

"Not yet."

"I think you might let me have a bit of chocolate. I might be blown up any minute, an' you'd be jolly sorry afterwards that you'd not let me have a bit of chocolate."

Mr. Brown glanced up from his paper.

"Your nuisance value, William," he said, "is so inestimably high that I'm sure you're the last person in England Hitler would wish to bomb."

"I bet it's me he's tryin' to get all the time," said William. "I bet he's heard about this aeroplane I'm makin'."

"I'm going to go on knitting that blue jumper," said Ethel. "I still think it's the wrong blue, but the war's simply played havoc with shades."

"Will there be enough of that cold lamb for tomorrow, Emma?" said Mrs. Brown.

She and Emma were together supplying the place of Cook, and each treated the other with pitying contempt as an amateur.

"Oh, yes, m'm. Lots," said Emma through the cork.

"I'll make a pie for the sweet," went on Mrs. Brown, "and we'll use up some of those pulped gooseberries."

"No need for you to do that, m'm," said Emma, removing the cork, her eyes gleaming with the light of battle. "I'll have ample time to run up a suet pudden. The master always likes my suet puddens."

"Very well, Emma," said Mrs. Brown, retreating, "but those pulped gooseberries aren't keeping any too well."

"One of them war-time recipes," said Emma with a grimace expressing fastidious disgust. "I've never trusted 'em. I warned both you an' Cook at the time, m'm if you remember."

With that she replaced her cork in a manner to preclude all further argument.

"Can I have the air-cushion, Mother?" said William.

"What for?"

"To—to rest on," said William. "My back aches."

"Well, you know you broke the last one with playing with it. You can have it on condition you don't play with it."

"All right, I don't want it, then," said William.

"And what *have* you got in your dressing-gown pocket?" Mrs. Brown leant forward and drew out a length of string, a penknife, a lump of putty, a handful of marbles, some screws, a matchbox containing a live beetle, and a tube of glue, most of whose contents had already escaped.

"Don't let the beetle out," said William anxiously. "It's one of the best I've ever had. I'm jus' goin' to give it a bit of biscuit."

"If anyone lets it out, I'll *die*," threatened Ethel.

"The glue's simply *soaked* through your dressing-gown," said Mrs. Brown. . . . "Oh, well," resignedly, "I can't do anything about it now. . . . Do stop eating biscuits, William. You've had quite enough."

"I bet that was a screaming bomb," said William.

"It was the twelve-thirty letting off steam," said Mr. Brown.

"Was it?" said William despondently. "It's been a rotten raid so far."

"I wonder if the Bevertons are coming," said Ethel.

"The *who*?" said Mr. Brown, looking up from his paper.

Ethel and Mrs. Brown exchanged nervous glances.

"Yes, didn't we tell you, dear?" said Mrs. Brown. "The Bevertons asked if they could share our shelter and we didn't like to say 'no'."

"Good heavens! They've got one of their own."

"I know, but they say it's so much jollier to be together. They were sharing the Mertons' last week, but Bella quarrelled with Dorita so they asked if they could share ours."

"SO SORRY WE'RE LATE," SAID MRS. BEVERTON GAILY
AS SHE ENTERED.

"Bella?" demanded Mr. Brown.

"Bella Beverton, dear," explained his wife. "One of Ethel's friends. Don't you remember her?"

"Ethel's friends are indistinguishable," said Mr. Brown. "Their vocabulary is limited to the word 'marvellous', but they can say it in twenty different tones of voice. Why intensify the horrors of war by having them in the air-raid shelter?"

"Perhaps they won't come, dear," said Mrs. Brown soothingly. "After all, it's some time since the siren went."

"They always take a long time getting ready," said Ethel.

"Ready? What for?" said Mr. Brown.

"For air-raid shelters," said Ethel.

"GOSH!" SAID WILLIAM EXCITEDLY. "I CAN HEAR BOMBS." BUT IT WAS ONLY THE BEVERTONS ARRIVING.

"Gosh," said William excitedly. "I can hear bombs." But it was only the Bevertons arriving.

Mrs. Beverton was inordinately stout and her daughter was inordinately thin. They were both dressed in the

latest in siren suits, and had obviously taken great pains
with their make-up and coiffeurs. Mrs. Beverton wore a
three-stringed pearl necklace, large jade ear-rings and
four bracelets. She had, moreover, used a new exotic
perfume that made William cry out in genuine alarm
"Gas! Where's my gas mask?"

"So sorry we're late," she said gaily as she entered.
"We just had to finish off our new siren suits. We've
been working on them all day but they just needed the
finishing touches, as it were. I had to get out my
jewellery, too. I always like to feel I've got it with me, as
it were. Room for a little one?"

She plunged down on to a small camp mattress next
to Mr. Brown, almost blocking him from view.

"Not squashing you, I hope?" she inquired politely.

"Not at all," came the muffled voice of Mr. Brown
from between her and the wall of the shelter.

Bella sat down by Ethel and took out her knitting.
"I'm making a green jumper like that one of yours," she
said. "Did you get your perm?"

"Yes. Yesterday."

"I'll have to have another soon if the raids keep on."

"Now you'd all like something to eat and drink,
wouldn't you?" said Mrs. Brown happily, setting to
work on her tea equipage and adding almost mechan-
ically, "I do hope Robert's all right."

"Do you like this colour?" said Ethel, holding up the
jumper she was working on.

"Marvellous!" said Bella in a deep voice.

"I want to get it finished by to-morrow. I like the yoke
effect, don't you?"

"Marvellous!" said Bella on a higher key.

"Did you see the cardigan Dolly Clavis knitted, with a
hood? She's going to lend me the pattern. It'll be useful
for cold mornings."

"*Marvellous!*" squeaked Bella ecstatically.

"You'll have a cup of tea, won't you, dear?" said Mrs. Brown to her husband.

But Mr. Brown wasn't there. At Bella's third "*Marvellous!*" he had crept quietly out of the emergency exit.

"Isn't he *tiresome!*" sighed Mrs. Brown. "Now, William, you can have one more biscuit and then you must lie down and try to sleep."

"Sleep!" echoed William indignantly, but his eyelids were heavy and it was all he could do to keep them open.

Mrs. Beverton had embarked upon a sea of prattle. "This scrap-iron business is simply disgraceful," she said. "It's the same everywhere. They made a terrific effort just at the beginning and then let things slide. There must be lots more scrap iron about by now that no one's troubled to collect."

William gradually surrendered to the tide of sleep that was engulfing him. Through it he heard an occasional "Marvellous!" from Bella, or a "I do hope that Robert and your father are all right" from his mother.

He slept through the All Clear but was roused by Mrs. Brown. He gathered his scattered pieces of aeroplane sleepily together.

Mrs. Beverton was still in full sail on her sea of prattle.

"This cousin of mine", she was saying, "made quite a little sum for the Spitfire Fund by this exhibition—just bits of shrapnel and a piece of a Dornier, and part of a shell-casing and a German incendiary bomb and a few things like that. People paid a shilling admission and she's promised to lend it to me and——"

Mrs. Brown smothered a yawn.

"That was the 'All Clear'," she said. "Shall we go back to bed?"

"What a shame!" said Mrs. Beverton. "I always hate leaving a party."

Ethel sat up and rubbed her eyes.

"We had quite a nice little nap," she said to Bella, "didn't we?"

"Marvellous," yawned Bella.

* * *

As William, back in his own bed, yielded once more to sleep, his thoughts went over what Mrs. Beverton had been saying just before he went to sleep in the shelter. No one was collecting scrap iron . . . people ought to be collecting scrap iron . . . people ought to be . . . people ought to . . . people ought. . . . He fell asleep and dreamed that Hitler, wearing Mrs. Beverton's siren suit, and Emma (still with the cork in her mouth) were wheeling a handcart of scrap iron, which turned into a gigantic aeroplane in the shape of a beetle which turned into Farmer Smith's Daisy.

He awoke with the firm conviction that he must do something about scrap iron.

Most of his previous war efforts had been unsuccessful, but, he decided, they had, perhaps, been too ambitious. He had tried to capture spies and parachutists, and this had turned out to be more difficult than he had thought it would. He couldn't go wrong collecting scrap iron. Nobody could go wrong collecting scrap iron. . . . You just—well, you just collected scrap iron, and then took it to the depot in Hadley.

He remembered that the organisers of the original appeal for scrap iron had had notices printed and dropped through letter-boxes, asking people to collect their scrap iron and advising them that it would be called for on a certain day. That, then, obviously, was the way to set about it. . . .

He assembled his Outlaws that morning and expounded his scheme to them.

"We'll write notices," he said, "and put them into people's letter-boxes, an' then, when they've had time to get the scrap iron together, we'll go round an' collect it. We can use my wooden cart or a wheelbarrow or somethin'. An' I bet they'll be jolly grateful to us ."

The composition of his "appeal" took some time, as none of them could remember exactly how the original one had been worded. The final effort was chiefly William's.

SKRAPPION

Plese collect your skrappion and we will call for it tomorro.

By order, William Brown.

They spent several hours copying it out and took it round the village in the evening.

There was another air-raid alarm that night, and again Mrs. Beverton and Bella joined the Browns in their shelter. Again Mrs. Beverton prattled merrily all night. This time she knitted as well, taking up, as it seemed, almost the entire shelter with elbow acrobatics and running a knitting needle into Mr. Brown's eye three or four times before he finally took to flight. Again Bella said "Marvellous!" fifty times in fifty different tones of voice. Again Emma wore her cork, taking it out only to snub Mrs. Brown when she suggested making a milk pudding for lunch the next day. Again the only recognisable sounds outside the shelter were the distant lowing of Daisy and an occasional motorist.

William busied himself with his aeroplane and his plans for collecting scrap iron. He was vaguely aware that Mrs. Beverton was prattling about a Spitfire Fund exhibition, and asking his mother to tea the next day, but was too much occupied with his own affairs to listen to her.

The next afternoon the Outlaws set off to collect the scrap iron. The result was at first disappointing. People were either amused or annoyed but in neither case did they produce any scrap iron. Mrs. Monks they found specially irritating.

"No, children," she said firmly, "we can't be bothered to play games with you now. We have work to do for the country even if you haven't," and vanished before they could explain that they had come on a matter of urgent national importance.

By the time they reached Miss Milton's they were definitely discouraged. Miss Milton was discouraging at the best of times, and in view of their treatment by normally quite pleasant people they felt that it would be worse than useless to present themselves at the front door and demand scrap iron. They were, however, reluctant to leave the house without making some effort towards the attainment of their object.

"Let's go round to the back," suggested William. "I believe I remember seein' a lot of rubbish behind her toolshed. Her gardener found 'em in that bit of waste ground he was clearin' for the potatoes."

They went round to the back and peeped over the hedge. Yes, there was the little heap of scrap iron that William remembered having seen—battered saucepans, rusty tin cans, old kettles. . . .

"Crumbs!" said William. "That's just what we want. An' *she* can't want it." He glanced at the house. "We won't bother her goin' to ask her. We'll jus' take it through the hedge. I bet that's the best thing to do. I bet she'd rather we did that than come to the house an' bother her. . . . I'll get through and hand it out to you."

He scrambled through the hedge and handed the pieces of scrap iron one by one to the others. They almost—not quite—filled the handcart.

"That's jolly good," said William as they set off again. "I bet she'll be jolly grateful to us when she finds out. Let's try Mrs. Beverton next," he suggested. "She comes to our air-raid shelter, an' my father says she's worse than the air raid, but I bet she'll have a bit of scrap iron. I put one of the notices through her letter-box, anyway."

They trundled the cart along to Mrs. Beverton's house, opened her small front gate and wheeled it up the path towards the front door. And then William suddenly stopped. For the french windows of the morning-room were open and inside the morning-room, on a long trestle table, was what could be nothing other than a collection of scrap iron kindly left there for them by Mrs. Beverton.

"*Corks!*" gasped William. "That's jolly decent of her. She's jus' left 'em there ready for us so's we could get 'em without botherin' her. It's *jolly* decent of her."

He wheeled the cart across the lawn, put it down beside the french windows, and entered the morning room.

The collection of scrap iron was certainly impress-ive—heavy pieces of metal, jagged pieces of metal, dull pieces of metal, pieces of metal of all textures, shapes and sizes.

"There's not room for it all in the cart," said Ginger.

"No, but it's a jolly sight better than that stuff of ole Miss Milton's," said William. "It's jolly good scrap iron, an' it's jolly decent of her to put it out ready for us like this. I'd like to take it to Hadley first, before Miss Milton's. They'll be jolly pleased with it down at Hadley. I bet it'll be the best they ever had. . . . I say! We could leave Miss Milton's ole stuff here, an' take this down to Hadley an' then come back for Miss Milton's, couldn't we? I bet that's a jolly good idea. . . . Come on, let's

"*CORKS!*" GASPED WILLIAM. "IT'S *JOLLY* DECENT OF HER," THE
COLLECTION OF SCRAP IRON WAS CERTAINLY IMPRESSIVE.

take Miss Milton's out an' put this in. This'll just fill the
cart nicely, an' then we can get a bit more to put with ole
Miss Milton's an' make up the second cartful. Come
on. . . ."

In a few minutes they had emptied the cart, put its
contents on the trestle table, and put the contents of the
trestle table into the cart.

Then, with the pleased feeling of a patriotic duty
satisfactorily accomplished, they set off to Hadley.

* * *

Mrs. Beverton's preparations for the Spitfire Exhibition tea party were somewhat behindhand. She had taken her afternoon nap, as usual, and overslept, so that she was still harassing her little maid over the arrangements for tea when the guests were due to arrive.

Moreover, Bella, who was supposed to have copied out the labels for the exhibits, so kindly lent by Mrs. Beverton's cousin, had forgotten all about it, and was now hastily scribbling them upstairs in her bedroom. Bella was feeling rather disgruntled, firstly because she had not heard from her latest boyfriend for over a week and secondly because she was beginning to have a horrible suspicion that the green jumper didn't suit her. So, though everything was still "Marvellous", it was marvellous in a minor key.

"Bella, *do* hurry up with those labels," called Mrs. Beverton from downstairs. "I thought you'd have got them done this morning."

"I was busy," said Bella petulantly. "I was finishing that wretched jumper. I think it's a frightful colour."

"Well, you would have it," said Mrs. Beverton unsympathetically.

"I know. It looked all right on Ethel."

"Oh, well, any colour suits Ethel," said Mrs. Beverton. "She's so pretty."

"Marvellous," said Bella tartly.

"Now do hurry up with those labels, dear. I can't think why you've been so long."

Bella muttered something under her breath that certainly wasn't "Marvellous", and scrawled the remaining half-dozen labels.

"I've finished them now, Mother."

"Well, I wish you'd go and put them on the exhibits in the morning-room, dear. It's after four, and I've still got to change."

"But I don't know which to put on which," objected Bella.

"You can't go wrong, dear. I've put them in a straight line in order all along the table and the labels are numbered. Just put label No. 1 on the one nearest the door and so on to the window. You can't go wrong, and I'm sure it's nice for you to feel that you're helping Mother."

"Marvellous!" said Bella in what she imagined to be a tone of cutting irony.

She took the labels down to the morning-room. She was still feeling aggrieved by her mother's reference to Ethel Brown. She never had been able to understand what people saw in Ethel Brown. Personally she thought that Ethel looked a perfect sight in the green jumper. She never had liked her hair. Or her voice. Or her eyes. . . .

She stood in the doorway of the morning-room and looked with dispassionate contempt at the collection of metal on the table. . . . It was the first time she had seen it (she had been out when it arrived) and it was, she thought, a pretty rotten show. It wasn't in a straight line either, whatever her mother might say. She straightened it and began to put the labels round. "Part of wing of Messerschmitt" (looked more like a rusty old saucepan). "Piece of shell casing" (looked more like an old kettle lid—what you could see of it for rust). "Part of aileron from Dornier 17" (more like an old sardine tin). She flung the labels down anyhow one by one. There were too many labels for the exhibits but she didn't care. She wasn't interested in the rotten old exhibition, and she didn't care whether it was a success or not. After all, one would expect one's own mother to appreciate one's good points if no one else did. She had always thought that her hair, especially after a brightening shampoo, was a better colour than Ethel Brown's any day. . . .

Mrs. Beverton had changed into her mauve georgette just in time breathlessly to receive the first guest. There were so few social activities of any kind nowadays that all the invitations she sent out had been accepted even at such short notice. Mrs. Monks was coming and Miss Milton and Mrs. Bott and Mrs. Clavis and Mrs. Barton and Mrs. Brown and Miss Blake and Miss Featherstone.

Mrs. Beverton hurried breathlessly down to the drawing-room just as the little maid was admitting Mrs. Barton. One by one but almost immediately afterwards (for the meaningless urban convention of arriving everywhere half an hour late was rightly held in scorn here) the others arrived.

"Do come in," said Mrs. Beverton brightly as she ushered them into the drawing-room. "So nice of you to come to my little party. All in a good cause, isn't it? I thought that we'd have tea first and that while we were having it you could go one by one and see the exhibition. There really isn't room in the morning-room for all of us. I've put a plate on the table near the door, and if you'll all put your sixpence in that—or however much more you like to make it, of course. . . . All the exhibits are numbered and described. Will you go first, Miss Featherstone? You know where the morning-room is, don't you? Just across the way. . . ."

Miss Featherstone went out, and the others sat down and began tea. In a short time Miss Featherstone returned. She looke pale and bewildered.

"Well," said Mrs. Beverton with a complacent and expectant smile, "did you find it interesting?"

"Er—yes," said Miss Featherstone uncomfortably, avoiding her hostess's eye. "Er—y-yes."

"Tragic, of course, I agree," said Mrs. Beverton. "Definitely tragic, of course. I quite understand how you feel. I'm not one to gloat over it myself. However you look at it, it means tragedy in one form or another. . . . Now, Miss Blake, would you like to see it? Just pop your sixpence on to the plate. Or a bit more, of course, if you really like the show. . . . You know the way to the morning-room, don't you? . . . A little more tea, Mrs. Brown?"

A few moments later Miss Blake returned to the room. She, too, looked pale and bewildered.

"Well?" said Mrs. Beverton again expectantly. "It's interesting, isn't it?"

Miss Blake avoided both her hostess's eye and Miss Featherstone's as she stammered, "Er—yes," and returned to her seat.

Mrs. Beverton looked from her to Miss Featherstone in surprise. How odd people were nowadays! No interest in anything—not even a Spitfire Fund Exhibition. It must be the war, of course, and lack of sleep. . . . She was glad it hadn't taken her like that.

One by one the other guests went in to see the exhibition, and all returned with that same air of bewilderment, that constrained and embarrassed manner.

"What do you think of it?" murmured Mrs. Clavis to Mrs Barton under cover of the general conversation. "Do you think that the war's turning her peculiar?"

"Well, the whole thing's most extraordinary," said Mrs. Barton. "I can only put it down to lack of sleep. I hardly like to think it's a deliberate trick."

"I'm not so sure," said Mrs. Clavis darkly. "I'm really not so sure."

"Odd that no one's *said* anything."

"Well, one doesn't like to. I didn't give any money, did you?"

"Indeed, I did not," said Mrs. Barton. "The thing's a deliberate fraud. At least it's a fraud; whether deliberate or not, it's not for me to decide."

"I should think that Mrs. Monks would *say* something," said Miss Blake hopefully. "I mean, it's supposed to be the duty of the church to speak *out*."

Mrs. Monks was at that moment entering the room, and it was quite clear that she was going to "speak out". She stood just inside the drawing-room door, fixing her eyes on Mrs. Beverton in dramatic denunication.

"Mrs. Beverton," she said in the voice that she generally kept for unruly choirboys. "Mrs Beverton, I cannot allow you to continue this gross deception."

Mrs. Beverton gaped at her.

"Th-th-th-th-this what?" she said.

"This gross deception," repeated Mrs. Monks. "This obtaining of money under false pretences for *whatever* purpose."

"I—I don't understand you," stammered Mrs. Beverton. "Really, Mrs. Monks, I know that we're *all* suffering from lack of sleep, but——"

"Your exhibition is nothing but a collection of scrap iron of a particularly valueless description."

"How *dare* you?" said Mrs. Beverton. "This collection was lent me by my cousin. She made two pounds, six shillings and tenpence halfpenny by it for her local Spitfire Fund, and you have the impertinence to say——"

Miss Milton now appeared in the doorway. She, too, had been in to see the "Exhibition". Her small precise figure quivered with indignation.

"This is an outrage, Mrs. Beverton," she said.

Mrs. Beverton gazed helplessly from one to the other. *Two* of them suffering from delusions as a result of lack of sleep. . . .

"What on *earth* do you mean, Miss Milton?" she said.

"I know that we've had to spend most of the nights in our

shelter lately, and I know that——"

"You must be aware", said Miss Milton, "that your so-called exhibition is merely a collection of scrap iron purloined by means I do not understand from the back of my toolshed?"

"You're mad," said Mrs. Beverton. "You *must* be mad."

"I recognise every single piece," said Miss Milton grimly. "There's the old fish slice that I threw away because it was too small, and that you have the impertinence to label as part of a Dornier wing. There's that old saucepan that leaks and I had soldered twice, and that you've labelled as a German incendiary bomb. The whole thing is beneath contempt and an insult to our intelligence. It——"

Dazedly Mrs. Beverton appealed to the others, but to her amazement they supported her accusers. They hadn't liked to *say* anything, but—well, Miss Milton and Mrs. Monks were quite right. It was just a collection of scrap iron. They didn't know how Mrs. Beverton had the face to play such a trick on them.

"This is a conspiracy," said Mrs. Beverton dramatically. "Nothing other than a conspiracy."

She swept into the morning-room, followed by her bewildered guests. At the door she stopped and stared at the line of rusty battered metal on the table.

"It's a German plot," she gasped. "It's the work of someone who wants to stop the money going to the Spitfire Fund." Her eyes roved accusingly over her guests. "One of you must be responsible. It was a genuine exhibition before you came, wasn't it, Bella?"

"Oh, no, Mother," said Bella calmly, "it wasn't. It was just like this."

"*What?*" said Mrs. Beverton, clutching her head with both hands. "Am I mad or are you?"

"Well, I'm not," said Bella calmly.

At this point the little maid entered.

"It's that there William Brown, 'm," she said. "He says, thank you very much for the scrap iron an' he's come back for the lot he left here."

"Oh dear, oh dear, oh dear!" groaned Mrs. Brown. "I had a *feeling* all along that William was at the bottom of it."

"How simply marvellous!" squeaked Bella.

* * *

Mr. Brown assumed his sternest expression when Mrs. Brown laid the story before him that evening.

"I quite agree with you, my dear," he said. "The boy's getting hopelessly out of hand. Just because there's a war on he thinks he can be allowed to go about making a nuisance of himself to everyone. He needs a lesson, and I'll see that he gets it."

"It was dreadful," moaned Mrs. Brown, "and then when Mrs. Beverton said in front of everyone that she wouldn't dream of using our air-raid shelter any more, I felt——"

"Said *what*?" demanded Mr. Brown.

"That she wouldn't dream of using our air-raid shelter any more."

"She—actually—said—that?" asked Mr. Brown slowly.

"Yes. In fact she made arrangements then and there to join the Bartons."

The look of severity faded from Mr. Brown's face. As far as a face of his particular cast of grimness could be said to shine, it shone.

"So—she won't be coming if there's a raid to-night?"

"No, dear. But about William——"

"Yes, yes," said Mr. Brown impatiently. "The boy

obviously meant no harm. I can't see what you're making all this fuss about. Actually, when you come to think of it, he was trying to help. I can't understand why you're so hard on the child."

"But——" began Mrs. Brown.

"You're quite *sure* that the Bevertons aren't coming again?"

"Quite, dear."

An almost seraphic smile spread over Mr. Brown's countenance.

"How marvellous!" he quoted.

Chapter 8

William Helps the Spitfire Fund

"No, I won't," said Mrs. Bott. "I won't an' that's that."

The "Dig for Victory" committee—consisting of Mr. Brown, General Moult, Mr. Monks, Mr. Luton, Mr. Barton and Mr. Flowerdew—exchanged glances of hopelessness and irritation. They'd been at it for more than an hour, and they were all getting a bit tired. . . .

"But, listen, Mrs. Bott——" said Mr. Brown.

"I 'ave listened," snapped Mrs. Bott. "I've 'eard all you've got to say, an' I won't 'ave it an' that's flat."

"But, Mrs. Bott," said Mr. Luton, "all we're asking is that you let us have your park for allotments. The men won't come through your garden or annoy you in any way. They'll come in, of course, by the gate from the main road. It's the only suitable piece of land in the neighbourhood."

"Yes, an' what about me an' Botty?" said Mrs. Bott indignantly. "Right up to our winders that park comes, remember. What about me an' Botty with a lot of common men trampin' about just outside the 'ouse an' starin' in at us when we're 'avin' our meals? D'you think me and Botty paid all that money for the 'All to 'ave common people trampin' about just outside same as if we'd never got on in the world?"

"But, Mrs. Bott," said Mr. Monks in his turn, "you must realise that this is of vital national importance.

Need we remind you that we're at war and——?"

"No, you need *not* remind me that we're at war." retorted Mrs. Bott, compressing her small, tight lips till they almost vanished into her chubby cheeks. "D'you think with things the price they are I need reminding of *that*? Wicked, it is! Why, only las' week I couldn't get any bacon—not the sort Botty likes for his breakfast, anyway. Nor any smoked salmon that both Botty an' me's partial to. An' these 'ere tradespeople what used to be so polite—well, off 'and's not the word. 'Take it or leave it,' they 'ave the cheek to say. No, you needn't tell *me* there's a war on."

They looked at her in silence. It was well known that Mr. Bott (affectionately referred to as "Botty" by his spouse), the present owner of the Hall, had made an immense fortune out of Bott's Digestive Sauce, and was not doing too badly in the way of war contracts.

"Perhaps if Mr. Bott——" began Mr. Barton tentatively.

"Botty's away on business," said Mrs. Bott sharply, "but we talked it over before 'e went, an' 'e agrees with me."

The committee sighed. The lady spoke the truth. Never yet had "Botty" been known to disagree on any point with his good lady.

"Trampin' about outside our very windows," repeated Mrs. Bott with growing indignation. "Starin' in at us 'avin' our meals. . . ."

"We'll do everything possible to meet that objection," said Mr. Flowerdew. "A fence or a hedge. . . . Certainly the men will not be allowed to come within a certain distance of the house. The——"

"No, *thanks*," snapped the lady. "I've always wanted to live in a big 'ouse with a park an' I'm *goin'* to live in a big 'ouse with a park. I *'ate* allotments. I always 'ave an' I always will. Nasty common crowded-up things! As for vegs., me an' Bott never 'ave cared for 'em. Rather 'ave somethin' tasty any day. I tell you, it'd fair take my appetite away to see a lot of common people diggin' whenever I looked out of the winder."

"Of course, if official pressure were brought to bear——" suggested Mr. Brown suavely.

Mrs. Bott's small eyes gleamed with rage.

"You try what you calls hofficial pressure on me, Mr. John Brown," she said, "an' I cancels hevery single subscription I gives to this 'ere bloomin' village!"

Mr. Brown coughed and subsided. The lady had them there and knew it. Difficult though she was, she contributed generously to the funds of the various local organisations, which would have been hard put to it to carry on without her.

"There's nothing more to be said, then?" said Mr. Flowerdew, rising.

"No, there ain't!" said Mrs. Bott. "I'm not 'avin' my park turned into no common allotments an' that's flat. You can put that in your pipe an' smoke it."

"I can hardly believe, Mrs. Bott, that your decision is final," said General Moult, making a last effort and assuming an expression of ferocity that had, in its time, caused many a recruit and even subaltern to tremble. It glanced off Mrs. Bott like a pin off a tank.

"Yes, it is," she said, "an' don't try comin' it over me with your harmy hairs an' graces."

General Moult, on hearing one of his most famous disciplinary measures described as "harmy hairs an' graces", sat down again and appeared to gasp for breath while the good lady continued: "An' I don't want no one muckin' about in my park—not you nor no one. A hornamental pleasure park it was described in the advert., an' a hornamental pleasure park it's goin' to stay. And now git out, all of you. . . ."

She advanced upon them, cheeks flushed, eyes alight with battle, and the "Dig for Victory" committee, headed by General Moult, who in his youth had faced hordes of charging Zulus unperturbed, turned ignominiously to flight.

MRS. BOTT ADVANCED UPON THEM, CHEEKS FLUSHED, EYES ALIGHT WITH BATTLE.

*   *   *

William was at home when his father and Mr. Flowerdew arrived. He listened absently as they reported the result of their mission to Mrs. Brown, using such expressions as "lack of public spirit", "fifth columnist", "disgraceful anti-British behaviour", which they had not dared to use to the lady's face.

"Isn't there any other piece of land round about that would do?" inquired Mrs. Brown.

Evidently there wasn't. Most of the once unoccupied land was now "taken over by the military" for camps or extensions of Marleigh Aerodrome, and the Hall park

THE "DIG FOR VICTORY" COMMITTEE, HEADED BY GENERAL MOULT, TURNED IGNOMINIOUSLY TO FLIGHT.

remained the only piece of land suitable for allotments for the people of Hadley and district.

But William was not really interested in all this.

William was worried. A heavy load of guilt rested on his conscience. Without meaning to—certainly without meaning to—he had completely ruined Mrs. Beverton's Spitfire Fund Exhibition by exchanging it for a collection of old iron. . . .

Mrs. Beverton's cousin had made £2 6*s*. 10½*d*. by her collection. Mrs. Beverton, though perhaps she would not have made quite so much as that, would still have made something. . . .William, whose efforts to bring about a successful conclusion of the war had been unrelaxing if not always fortunate, felt it intolerable that he should have been the means of robbing the Spitfire Fund of a possible £2 6*s*. 10½*d*. He felt like a boy under a curse. For the first time since the poem had been set as a holiday task by a callous form master, he appreciated the feelings of "The Ancient Mariner". . . . But William was not a boy to labour under a sense of guilt without doing something to extirpate it. He got up suddenly while his father was calling Mrs. Bott a "dratted old termagant" and went round to collect his Outlaws from their various homes. Their steps led them almost automatically to their usual meeting-place at the old barn, and there William propounded his plan.

"We messed up Mrs. Beverton's Spitfire Fund Exhibition," he said, "an' so I votes we have one of our own to make up to her."

"We've not got any things for it," objected Ginger, "an' she had to send hers home to her cousin the same day, you remember."

"Yes, but we can *get* things, can't we?" said William impatiently.

"We can't get bits of Dorniers an' things same as she had," pointed out Henry.

"No," admitted William, "I s'pose we can't. But—tell you what—we'll call it a War Museum an' get all the things we can c'nected with the war."

"What sort of things?" said Douglas.

William considered.

"Well, we've got bits of shrapnel, haven't we?"

"There's not much in a bit of shrapnel," said Ginger gloomily. "Everyone's got a bit of shrapnel. No one'll pay to see anyone else's."

"Well, there's other things we can get."

"What other things?"

"Well . . . there's—there's—well, we'll jus' have to have a look round. Robert's got a bit of German parachute cord, but I bet he won't lend it me, an' I don't know where he keeps it."

"An' my father's got the end of a German bomb-stick," said Henry, "but I bet *he* won't lend it. They're all so jolly mean with their things."

"Well, I votes we go out an' have a look round," said William hopefully. "We might sort of find something."

There was a short pause, then he continued:

"Tell you what. We'll put up a notice on the door, 'War Museum Entrance 6*d*. Open 2.30,' an' I bet we'll 've found somethin' jolly int'restin' by 2.30. . . . Henry and Douglas can stay here an' 'splain to anyone what comes along that the Museum things'll be here in a minute an' Ginger 'n' me'll go an' find somethin'."

Infected, as usual, by William's optimism, the Outlaws helped him fix up the notice, then he and Ginger sallied forth in search of suitable exhibits, while Henry and Douglas stayed to prepare the old barn for the Museum and if possible attract patrons.

"What about a bit of tree knocked down by German aeroplane?" said Ginger, picking up a piece of wood from the road. "After all, we've got no proof it *wasn't*."

After some discussion, however, they decided not to resort to such dubious means for filling the Museum.

"No, we've gotter find somethin' *real*," said William. "Come on. I bet we'll soon find somethin' real. After all, there's a war on. We oughter be able to find *somethin'* to do with it if we look hard enough."

They were passing a stile leading to a path over the field which was blocked by a large notice, "Unexploded Bomb". The notice had been there for the past three weeks and at first the Outlaws had spent the greater part of each day standing in front of it and trying to circumvent the policeman whose duty it was to guard the path, in order to make closer investigation. Latterly, however, they had lost interest in it, for it was now generally known that the unexploded bomb was a "dud", and, though the notice still stood there, the field path was again in general use.

"It *would* be a dud," said William morosely as they passed. "We never have any luck here!"

At that moment a policeman came up and began to move the board on to one side.

"What're you doing?" said William, a little resentfully.

William was conservative by nature, and the notice had become one of the landmarks of the countryside.

"Orders," said the policeman. "Takin' of it away. At least movin' it from the path. It ain't 'arf 'eavy neither."

The words "Unexploded Bomb" were painted in red on a heavy white-painted board supported by two wooden legs at either end. The policeman dragged it from the path and tipped it into the ditch so that it was concealed by the overhanging grass.

"It can stay there till this evenin'," he said. "They're sendin' a barrer for it this evenin'. Now, cut along, you nippers. Not enough to do, you 'aven't, that's what's wrong with you. 'Angin' about all day long. I was workin' when I was your age. . . ."

He mounted his bicycle, which he had propped up against the stile, and rode off pursued by indignant outcries from the Outlaws.

"*Work!*" said Ginger. "I bet no one's ever had to work like us before. Fancy callin' bein' a p'liceman work, anyway. I bet I'd rather be a p'liceman than have to do all the rotten ole homework we have to do. . . . Gosh! They don't know what work *is*, don't p'licemen jus' goin for nice walks all day same as if they was on holiday. Gosh! I wish I'd nothing to do all day but go for nice walks about the country, same as a policeman, 'stead of wearin' my brain out over sums an' suchlike. . . ."

He turned to William for support but William was staring down at the ditch, where the top of the "Unexploded Bomb" notice could just be seen.

"I say," said William thoughtfully, "it'd do jolly well for our War Museum."

"They wouldn't let us have it," said Ginger.

"They don't want it till they fetch it back this evenin'," said William. "He *said* they weren't comin' to fetch it till this evenin'. It couldn't do any harm to take it for the Museum this afternoon. We'd have it back by the time they came to fetch it. Come on! It'd make a jolly good beginning for the Museum an' then I bet we'll find somethin' else. . . ."

Together they dragged the board, with its trestle legs, out of the ditch and began to carry it along the road. They carried it for some distance then set it down.

"Gosh!" gasped William breathlessly. "It's jolly heavy, isn't it? Let's leave it here a minute an' go an' get Henry an' Douglas to help us."

They set it down in the road and went back to the old barn to fetch Henry and Douglas.

They did not realise that they had left the board in the road immediately at the gates of the Hall. It happened

THEY CARRIED IT FOR SOME DISTANCE THEN SET IT DOWN.
"GOSH!" GASPED WILLIAM BREATHLESSLY. "IT'S JOLLY HEAVY,
ISN'T IT?"

that no one passed for the next few minutes and that at
the end of the next few minutes Mrs. Bott came along.
She was returning home from a little tour of the village,
during which she had complained to the grocer and
complained to the baker and complained to the butcher
and complained to everyone she met. She had had, in
fact, quite a good morning and was feeling quite pleased
with herself as she waddled back along the road to the
gates of the Hall. And there she stopped abruptly, and

stood staring in incredulous horror, her face growing longer and paler each second. Now, though she could bully and bluster and put up a show of courage with the best, yet when it came to a question of her own personal safety, no more timid soul existed than Mrs. Bott. She stood staring at the notice for some seconds, her eyes and mouth open to their fullest extent, then turned and waddled down the road as quickly as she could. She arrived at the nearest house, which happened to be the Browns', panting and perspiring.

"Oh dear!" she gasped, sinking down on to a chair. "Oh dear! oh dear! oh dear! Oh, Mrs. Brown, what shall I *do*? a hunexploded bomb right in front of my very 'ouse. I daren't go in an' I don't know what's 'appened to poor Pussy, not to speak of the servants. Thank 'eaven Botty's not at 'ome. But—oh, to think it may be goin' up this very second, an' all the beautiful furniture an' jew'l'ry Botty's spent 'is money on all smithereens—not to speak of the servants. Oh dear, oh dear, oh dear!" She burst into sobs that shook her plump little form like a jelly. "Oh dear, whatever shall I do? 'Ow can I ever tell Botty that 'is beautiful 'ouse an' furniture an' poor Pussy an' the servants is blown up? Oh, Mr. Brown," as Mr. Brown, attracted by the uproar, came to see what was happening, "it's a judgement on me, I know it's a judgement on me! I did ought to've let you 'ave the park. I see it all plain now. If I 'ad done, this wouldn't never 'ave 'appened to me."

Mr. Brown went to the writing desk in the corner of the room and took out a paper.

"I have the document here," he said, "if you care to sign it. . . . Just there," he indicated.

"Oo, yes, I will," said Mrs. Bott eagerly. "Indeed I will. D'you think, if I do, nothin'll 'appen? I don't know what Botty paid for that furniture an' all them diamonds.

An' poor Pussy gets that put out when things don't go on same as usual. An' the servants an' all."

Her fat little hand guided the pen unsteadily but quite legibly over the line Mr. Brown pointed out.

"It gives us the use of the park for allotments for the duration of the war." said Mr. Brown, folding up the document. "The committee will be most grateful," he added.

"Really, John," said Mrs. Brown reproachfully, "you might do something about the bomb. Don't you see how upset poor Mrs. Bott is?"

Mr. Brown, like his younger son, had a one-track mind. He wanted Mrs. Bott's park for his allotments and couldn't think of anything else till he'd got it. Now that he'd got it, he could give his full attention to the lady's unexploded bomb.

"Let me get you some brandy," he said solicitously, "and I'll ring up the police at once."

He went out of the room to return a few moments later with the brandy, looking a little puzzled.

"The police say that there's no such board at your gates, Mrs. Bott," he said, "and that they've had no notice of any unexploded bomb in the neighbourhood at all."

"It was there," said Mrs. Bott in a tremulous voice as she sipped the brandy. "I seed it with me own heyes. Large as life. I'm still all of a turn. 'Ow I got 'ere I don't know. An' 'ow them there p'lice could deny it when——"

"You couldn't have imagined it?" suggested Mrs. Brown.

"Me imagine it!" repeated Mrs. Bott indignantly. "Me imagine a great board with 'Hunexploded bomb' on it in great red letters! No, Mrs. Brown, as true as I sits 'ere, I seed it. Seed it with me own heyes."

"I'll just go and take a look myself while you're recovering," said Mr. Brown.

"An' tell 'em to *do* somethin' about it," said Mrs. Bott, who was regaining something of her customary spirit. "Leavin' hunexploded bombs in people's private grounds! That 'Itler doesn't know where to stop, that's what's wrong with '*im*."

Some minutes later Mr. Brown returned to report that there was no sign of any notice of an unexploded bomb at the gates of the Hall. Mrs. Bott stared at him incredulously.

"But, I tell you, it *is* there," she said. "Din' you 'ear me tell you I seed it with me own heyes?"

"Well—suppose we all go and look at it together," suggested Mrs. Brown.

They walked down the road to the gates of the Hall, Mrs. Bott continued to assert that she'd seed it with her own heyes and to bemoan the fate of poor Pussy, the furniture and the servants.

At the gates she stopped abruptly and stood blinking.

"It *was* 'ere," she said in a low awestruck voice. "I tell you it *was* 'ere. Sure as my name's Maria, it *was* 'ere."

"But it's not here now," Mr. Brown assured her, "and it wasn't here when I came."

Mrs. Bott's expression changed to one of modest complacency.

"Things like that do 'appen to me," she said. "I'm what they call psysic."

"Psychic," murmured Mr. Brown.

"I 'ave warnin's," continued Mrs. Bott, ignoring him. "I 'ad one about the hair-raid shelter. I can what they call hinterpret of 'em, too. That one meant I'd gotter keep a heye on the lake, and this one meant I'd got to let you 'ave that land for allotments. Well, I done it, din' I?"

"You did," said Mr. Brown, "and the committee will be most grateful."

"Mind you, I'm goin' to like it, but", darkly, "there's worse'd come to me if I didn't. I know what a warnin' is. I've 'ad experience. That board was a vishun. The police say it wasn't there an' you say it wasn't there, but to me it *was* there. I don't s'pose you'd 'ave seen it if you'd been there with me. There's them as 'as the power of seein' vishuns an' there's them as 'asn't. Well, it's come to a choice of a lot of common people tramplin' about outside our very winders or the whole 'ouse blown up an' I think I've made the right choice."

"Indeed you have, Mrs. Bott," Mr. Brown assured her.

"Pussy'd never've got over it. Not to speak of the servants. . . . It doesn't bear thinkin' of. . . . Well, good day, an' thank you for all your kindness. I'll be gettin' on 'ome now."

*   *   *

Mrs. Bott spent the next few hours lying on her bed, recovering from the shock. When she got up, she thought she'd take another little stroll round the village. She still felt uplifted by the thought of her "gift", which enabled her to see notice-boards that were invisible to other people. "Psysic, that's what I am," she murmured complacently to herself as she waddled along. "It's a gift. It's——"

She stopped. A small boy was slouching past the Hall gates, hands deep in pockets, head sunk dejectedly. It was William. . . . The War Museum in aid of the Spitfire Fund had been a dismal failure. The "Unexploded Bomb" board had been the only exhibit, and things wouldn't have been any better had there been a more sensational display, as no one turned up to see it.

The organisers had waited till after tea-time, then returned the main feature of the unsuccessful "Exhibition" to its resting-place in the ditch.

Failure in any form was depressing enough, but failure in this case was particularly galling.

"Well now, whatever's the matter with *you?*" demanded Mrs. Bott with unusual cordiality. "You don't 'arf look gloomy."

"Me?" said William with a hollow laugh. "Me" I should think I *do* look gloomy. I've got a reason to look gloomy, I have."

"Why? What's happened?" said Mrs. Bott.

"I was havin' an exhibition for Mrs. Beverton's Spitfire Fund," said William, "an' no one came to it an' I've got no money for her."

"How much money did you want to make?" asked Mrs. Bott.

"Well, her cousin made £2 6s. 10½d. an' we wanted to make a bit more if we could."

Mrs. Bott opened her bag.

"As it 'appens," she said, "I've had a very wonderful hexperience. I might almost say the most wonderful deliverance. If I 'adn't been able to hinterpret it, my beautiful 'ouse might have bin in ruins this very minute. It was sent to tell me I'd gotter do more for the war. So", simply, "I *ham* doin' more. I've give my beautiful hornamental pleasure park for allotments, an' now I'm goin' to give you £3 for your Spitfire Fund."

William gasped. He held himself erect as though a load of guilt had rolled from his shoulders.

"*Gosh!*" he exclaimed. "That's *jolly* decent of you."

It was fortunate that it did not occur to William to describe to Mrs. Bott the nature of the only exhibit in his War Museum and that it did not occur to Mrs. Bott to describe to William the nature of her "experience".

The moment fraught with such dramatic possibilities passed safely in silence. . . .

Mrs. Bott handed him the three notes slowly one by one.

"*Thanks*," said William fervently. "I'll take them to Mrs. Beverton straight off."

Mrs. Bott heaved a deep sigh and looked about her.

"Well!" she said, "I oughter be safe for a bit now—Pussy an' all."

Chapter 9

William Gets a Move On

William wandered thoughtfully down the village street. After much consideration he had come to the conclusion that he wasn't doing enough to win the war. It was not that he didn't want to. It was that people wouldn't let him. . . . He'd tried every way he knew and been frustrated at every turn. He couldn't think why the many letters he had addressed to "The Guvnment London" offering his services as a spy (in Germany), a parashooter (in England), a parachutist (in Germany), and suggesting various ingenious devices for trapping tanks and submarines, had remained unanswered. True, he had not stamped them, but he had adorned the envelopes with the phrase "on His Majesty's Survise" written round and round the envelope in circles and occupying all the space not taken up by the actual address. He had written to several newspapers, urging that education was a waste of public money in the present crisis and that all schools should be closed, and the masters sent to work in the coal mines, but to his great disappointment none had been published. He had experimented with charcoal, sulphur and saltpetre in the greenhouse, hoping to discover some new explosive, but the only results had been a wrecked greenhouse, several minor injuries and the docking of his pocket-money for months to come. He thought bitterly of the different treatment accorded to other scientists who had risked their lives in such research.

"What about that man that 'sperimented with magnetic mines?" he demanded indignantly. "I bet no one stopped his pocket-money. An' I bet he made as much mess as what I did. Oh no, *he* gets a medal giv'n him an' I get into a row."

Yesterday he had watched some men removing sign-posts on the main road.

"Why don't you change 'em round 'stead of jus' takin' 'em away?" he had demanded. "Or else put up 'Egypt' or 'Russia' or somethin' to make 'em think they've come to the wrong country?"

The men refused to take his suggestions seriously, refused even to allow him to help, adding insult to injury by saying:

"We've no time to play games with nippers. There's a war on."

William walked on, feeling even more embittered than before. No one would accept his help. No one would take his advice. No one would even listen to him. . . .

"Don't see how they think they're goin' to win the war at this rate," he muttered morosely to a beech tree that grew on the roadside. "Jus' won't *listen* to people. I bet that was a jolly good idea. They could put a bit of sand about to make it look like Egypt or stick beards on to people to make it look like Russia. . . ."

Thinking over the matter, however, he had to admit that the transformation of the entire countryside to resemble distant continents might present some difficulties. Still—his first idea of changing the sign-posts round would have been quite easy, and the summary dismissal of his advice rankled.

"They'd 've landed in Marleigh an' thought they were

"WHY DON'T YOU CHANGE 'EM ROUND
'STEAD OF JUS' TAKING 'EM AWAY,"
WILLIAM DEMANDED.

in Hadley," he said, "an' I bet they'd 've got so muddled
they'd 've gone off home again."

The more he thought over the idea, the better it
seemed and the more outrageous appeared the behaviour of the men who had refused to adopt it.

"I bet they were Germans," he muttered. "I bet they
were spies an' columnists an' suchlike."

He walked on down the road, still meditating the
plan.

"They'd think they were in places where they weren't an' they'd get in an awful muddle, an'——"

He stopped. He was passing a house on whose gate was the name Heather Bank. The name was carved on a piece of wood, which was screwed on to the top rung of the gate. He remembered—almost subconsciously—having passed another house just outside Marleigh whose gate bore the name Laurel Bank carved and adjusted in just the same way. And—inspiration suddenly came to him. He couldn't change the sign-posts round, but he could alter the names of the houses. That would be almost as confusing to the enemy. . . . Only the other day he had heard someone say that the German parachutists were familiar with every inch of the English countryside, that they knew as much about each town and village as its own inhabitants knew. To change the names of the houses was almost as good as to change the sign-posts round. . . . If they came upon Heather Bank when they were expecting Laurel Bank they'd think they'd made a mistake and, with luck, go back to Germany again. William's spirits rose. Here at last was something he could do to win the war.

No one was in sight. He studied the name plate. . . . Yes, just ordinary screws. He'd go home and get a screw-driver.

When he returned, having "borrowed" a screw-driver from Robert's tool chest, he found the road still deserted. It was easier than he had imagined. He tucked "Heather Bank" under this arm and set off to "Laurel Bank". The two plates were identical in size and design. The owners, in fact, Colonel Peabody and Mr. Bagshott, had been devoted friends until a difference of opinion a few weeks ago had left them bitter enemies.

The difference of opinion, which, like most differences of opinion, had been essentially unimportant but had assumed gigantic proportions in the minds of the protagonists, had taken place in the Conservative club down in Hadley. Colonel Peabody—famous for miles round for his vegetable growing—had affirmed, in what Mr. Bagshott considered an offensively aggressive manner, that every inch of every garden should be dug up for vegetable growing. Mr. Bagshott, who carried off all local prizes for flowers, had taken the opposite view. He had insisted on the need of keeping up the standard of flower cultivation and on the importance of retaining our national reputation for beautiful gardens in order to help the nation's morale. The argument grew more and more heated on both sides. A more and more uncompromising attitude was adopted. The argument became more personal as it became more bitter. Colonel Peabody taunted Mr. Bagshott with the black spot that had blighted his roses for the past two seasons, and Mr. Bagshott taunted Colonel Peabody with the big-bud that had ruined his blackcurrants last year. Such references, of course, between friends are unforgivable. The two parted with flushed set faces and, the next time they met, passed each other with an almost imperceptible recognition. The second time they met they did not recognise each other. Each had brooded in the mean time, on the black-spot and big-bud insult respectively, till it had filled their entire horizon and they could think of nothing else. In the club they no longer sat side by side reading bits of the paper aloud to each other, no longer shared the same table when they lunched there. If Colonel Peabody saw Mr. Bagshott in the lounge he went to the writing-room, if Mr. Bagshott saw Colonel Peabody in the writing-room he went to the lounge. If Colonel Peabody saw that Mr. Bagshott was lunching at the club he went round to lunch at the Station Hotel. If Mr. Bagshott saw Colonel Peabody lunching at the Station Hotel he lunched at the club.

William, of course, busily engaged on changing the names that the two had ordered from the same firm in the same lettering in the days of their friendship, was wholly unaware of this situation. He had merely chosen these two particular houses because their name-plates were easy to interchange. He found the operation quite simple and, fortunately for him, the road remained deserted till he had completed it. Having completed it, he stood and looked at his work with a glowing sense of satisfaction. That'd muddle the old parachutists all right. They'd be looking for "Heather Bank" and see "Laurel Bank", or be looking for "Laurel Bank", and see "Heather Bank", and they'd think they'd come to the wrong place and go away. It might even win the war. . . . He swaggered homewards, smiling complacently to himself as if already receiving the plaudits of a grateful country.

The immediate task, however, was to return the screw-driver to Robert's tool chest before he noticed it had gone. Again luck was on his side. It wasn't till he'd put back the screw-driver and was going out again by the side door that he met Robert coming in.

"Where've you been?" demanded Robert in a tone of suspicious disapproval.

Robert's permanent attitude towards his younger brother was one of suspicious disapproval. This was partly the result of experience and partly the natural reaction of age to youth.

"Me?" said William airily. "Oh—I've just been round Marleigh."

Robert's face lost its line of stern aloofness and assumed that expression of soulful sentimentality that William had always characterised to himself as his "sick'nin' look".

"Did you—did you—pass Laurel Bank?" he asked, the soulful sentimentality of his expression verging on imbecility.

William remembered vaguely that the owner of Laurel Bank had a pretty niece staying with him to whom Robert had been vainly trying to obtain an introduction. The usual local festivities that could generally be trusted to introduce everyone to everyone else had ceased, of course, owing to the war, and Robert was in the unfamiliar and exasperating position of being in daily sight and sound of a pretty girl without being able to tell her how pretty she was. William decided that the less Robert knew of his recent activities the better.

He assumed his famous expression of bland bewilderment.

"Laurel Bank?" he said. "Where's Laurel Bank?"

"My goodness!" said the exasperated Robert. "Don't you know where Laurel Bank is? Are you blind?"

"Well, not quite," admitted William, "but I was saying to Father the other day that my eyes weren't too good an' I thought if I stopped at home from school a bit it'd give 'em a rest. P'raps," he ended hopefully, "if you'd tell him so, too——"

Robert strode from the room with an ejaculation of impatience.

* * *

But the thought of the fair unknown lingered on in Robert's mind. She had brown eyes, fair hair, a deliciously retroussé nose and was called Dulcie—an irresistible combination. He had managed to meet her in the village so often that she must have wondered why she could not step out of doors without encountering this moody-looking youth who fixed her with an ardent gaze and—for Robert always coughed when he was nervous—was evidently suffering from some deep-seated lung trouble.

He had walked round and round Laurel Bank till he felt dizzy without finding any opportunity of scraping acquaintance with her. Her uncle, when he met him, responded to his effusive greeting by a curt nod. Mr. Bagshott disliked young men at the best of times, and had never forgiven Robert for sending a tennis ball into his eye during a tennis tournament last summer.

Robert had, in fact, almost given up hope of bringing the affair to a satisfactory conclusion, when William's ignorance of the whereabouts of Laurel Bank stirred up all his interest afresh. He would walk in its direction just once more, he decided. . . . He would give fate just one more chance of helping him. He might find something going on that would give him an opportunity of introducing himself. . . .

What he actually found was an elderly but muscular gardener engaged in digging up the rose bed that contained Mr. Bagshott's prize roses. He had already dug up the herbaceous border that had been the joy and pride of Mr. Bagshott's heart. Plants and rose bushes were blazing merrily away on a bonfire.

Colonel Peabody had been brooding. He had brooded in fact day and night since the quarrel. He had thought of forceful arguments and telling repartees which he might have used and had not. He wasn't, of course, on speaking terms with old Bagshott now, so he couldn't continue the argument verbally. But he could—and must—continue it in deeds. At first he couldn't think what to do to show old Bagshott that he'd meant what he said. Then suddenly in the middle of the night as he was lying awake, brooding, an idea occurred to him. Although most of the garden was crammed with vegetables, there existed still—on sufferance, as it were—a dozen or so spindly rose trees and a few herbaceous plants that had managed to survive the general atmosphere of discouragement. He realised that their existence was an admission of weakness on his part, and a flat denial of his principles. Probably old Bagshott laughed every time he passed the place and saw them. They must come up. They must come up at once . . . . Not another day must pass before they came up. His own gardener, as it happened, was ill and he himself had a pressing engagement, so he rang up a firm of nurserymen in Hadley and asked them to send a man or men out to Heather Bank, to dig up the roses and herbaceous stuff and burn them. Thereupon, with a mind at rest and feeling that he had vindicated his principles and scored off old Bagshott, he set out for his engagement.

The man sent from Hadley did not know the neighbourhood, but he found the name Heather Bank on a gate soon after William had fixed it there, entered the garden and set to work. The rarity and splendour of the roses and herbaceous plants he had been ordered to demolish would have surprised him had he been a man who allowed anything to surprise him. He would have made further inquiries had he been a man who ever made further inquiries. But he was definitely not that sort of man. He was the sort of man who does what he has been told to do without question and without interest, and gets it done as quickly as possible. He had been told to dig up the roses and herbaceous plants, so he dug them up. He had been told to make a bonfire of them, so he made a bonfire of them. He dug up everything he could see and made a bonfire of it. As his orders had stated that the whole garden was to be prepared for vegetable planting, he started digging up the begonia bed. It was at this point that Robert appeared and saw the garden that had been its owner's joy and pride transformed to a patch of freshly dug earth. He leaned over the gate and gazed round in amazement. Then he looked at the house, and his face assumed the languishing expression that it always wore when he thought of Dulcie.

"Anyone at home?" he inquired of the digger.

The digger stopped digging and leaned upon his spade.

"No," he said, "family's out."

Then he spat and began to dig again.

Robert looked round again and his amazement increased.

"I say!" he said. "What are you doing!"

"Diggin' up garden," said the digger. "Takin' up all roses an' suchlike an' diggin' up garden."

"Why?" said Robert simply.

"Orders," said the man still more simply.

Robert's eyes looked on the scene of desolation again in fascinated horror. "Gosh!" he ejaculated at last on a note of awe.

The digger straightened himself and took out an ancient turnip watch.

"Time I knocked off, too," he said. "Back-achin' work, this 'ere!"

"D'you mean to say", said Robert incredulously, "that he *told* you to dig it up."

"Yep," said the man. "Dig it all up and sow vegs. Burns all roses an' suchlike. An' if he thinks I can do it in a day he's bats, that's what he is. My time's up and I'm goin'. Fair winded, I am. . . ."

"Did he want the whole—thing—dug—up?" said Robert.

"Yep . . . an' he wanted some veg. seed too. Gov'ner tol' me to give him these 'ere cat'logues." He drew a couple of crumpled catalogues from his pocket. "But, seein' as he's not 'ere, I can't."

"I'll take them," said Robert eagerly. "I'll take them and give them to him when he comes, and I'll go on with the digging, shall I?"

"Yer can if yer like to be such a fool," said the man without interest. "Don't make no difference ter me. I've broke my back enough for one day. . . . You can 'ave spade. It come out of toolshed. Well, good day to you. I'll go across to the pub for a pint, then get on 'ome."

With that he departed, leaving Robert in possession. Robert took off his coat, rolled up his sleeves, seized the spade and began to dig with zest. His zest declined somewhat as the moments passed and no one came, but still he dug on with unabated vigour. The glorious moment would arrive when Mr. Bagshott would appear at the gate, accompanied by the adorable Dulcie, and all would be gratitude and amiability. It wouldn't be difficult, perhaps, without any actual untruth, to give the impression that he'd done more digging than he actually had done. He might claim part of the rose garden and the herbaceous border. Anyway, Mr. Bagshott would have to ask him to tea. In very decency he'd have to ask him to tea. And the adorable Dulcie would smile on him (His heart throbbed at the prospect.) Then after tea he would do a little more digging, and Dulcie would watch him, admiring his strength and the rippling of his manly muscles under his bronzed skin. He pushed his shirt sleeves higher up and tried to make his muscles (which were, truth to tell, somewhat inadequate) ripple a little more manfully. It was at this moment that Mr. Bagshott appeared in the gateway. He stood there and his eyes roved round, at first with incredulity, then with horror, and finally with bloodshot rage. His rose garden—the pride of his heart—laid waste! His herbaceous border—

object of his fondest thoughts and dreams for years—ruined! His choicest plants blazing merrily away on a bonfire. And—originator presumably of the whole monstrous crime—that imbecile, young Brown, digging madly away on the spot where his treasured bed of begonias had been. Robert rested on his spade and smiled—a smile of simple pride and pleasure.

"Well, I've not done too badly, have I, sir?" he said.

Mr. Bagshott didn't speak. His mouth worked soundlessly, but he didn't speak. Dull blotches of red crept up from the region of his neck. Obviously words would come in time, and when they did they would be worth listening to. Robert gaped at him. He saw a man in the grip of some strong emotion. He took for granted at first that the emotion was gratitude . . . then he wasn't sure. The man, in fact, seemed to be angry. But what was there to be angry at? His orders had been carried out, his garden had been dug up, his plants had been burnt . . . and he, Robert, stood there—the central figure, the strong, silent digger who had accomplished the miracle, who had transformed the gay pleasure garden to this stark business-like expanse of brown earth. His gaze travelled to Dulcie whose face could be seen over her uncle's shoulder. It was pale and tense. Mouth and eyes were opened to their fullest extent. The girl was impressed. No doubt at all that the girl was impressed. Probably she took for granted that he'd dug up the whole thing. No need to disillusion her too much.

"I don't say I did it all, of course," he said modestly. "The other chap did some . . . but I did a good share of it."

Mr. Bagshott found his voice.

"D'you mean to say", he spluttered, "that *you've* done—this?"

"Oh, yes," admitted Robert carelessly. "Quite a good

deal of it, that is." He looked down at his muscles and tried once more to make them ripple. "I'm a good deal more powerful than I look. I——"

And then the full force of Mr. Bagshott's voice and vocabulary was restored. Robert blenched and staggered as the spate surged over him. Mr. Bagshott's vocabulary was a well-seasoned one at the best of times, and this afternoon he was like a man inspired. Never had he done it so much justice. At first Robert couldn't believe his ears, but finally he was driven to believe them despite himself. The words used by Mr. Bagshott were explicit beyond the possibility of misunderstanding. Such words as "ruffian", "hooligan", "Hun", "wanton destruction", "legal proceedings" cannot by the utmost stretch of imagination, even on the part of a love-bemused youth, be construed into expressions of gratitude.

"B-b-b-b-but," stammered Robert. "He said . . . you said. . . ."

"Get out," bellowed Mr. Bagshott, whose face was now one rich expanse of purple out of which his eyes gleamed like an enraged tiger's. "Get out. And I'll have you locked up for this, you blackguard. I'll—I'll—I'll—*Get out!*"

It was at this moment that Colonel Peabody appeared. His face, too, was purple with anger. He muttered savagely and made threatening lunges with his stick at the air as he walked.

Mr. Bagshott had only the other day come to the conclusion that the few vegetables that graced the tiny vegetable garden at the end of his herbaceous border must, after the quarrel they had had, give that fool Peabody a laugh every time he passed the place. The more Mr. Bagshott thought over this, the more bitter became his feelings. He didn't like vegetables, anyway,

IT WAS AT THIS MOMENT THAT COLONEL PEABODY APPEARED.

and he could never even give them away, because at the time his were ready to eat no one wanted them because theirs were ready too. Apart from everything else, vegetables never seemed to do well with him. His onions had been the size of peas last year, his carrots the size of pins. . . . He'd have the whole thing carted away and plant a few more roses. Then that ass Peabody would know that he meant what he had said. Having come to that conclusion, he couldn't let another day pass before putting the plan into execution and had called himself on one of the nurserymen in Hadley to ask them to send a man that afternoon to Laurel Bank to do it. The man had meant to ask for directions when he reached Marleigh but, happening to pass a house with Laurel

"GET OUT!" BELLOWED MR. BAGSHOTT AT ROBERT. "I'LL—
I'LL—I'LL—*GET OUT!*"

Bank on the gate, had entered and set to work. . . .

Colonel Peabody had come home to find roses and
herbaceous plants desecrating the garden that had
always been held sacred to vegetables. The gardener was
still there digging. He described the man who had given
the monstrous order and the description tallied so
exactly with Mr. Bagshott that it left no room for doubt.
Thereupon Colonel Peabody, too much excited to
notice that the name on the gate had been changed, set
off down the road to challenge the one-time friend who
had dared to put this intolerable affront upon him.

By the time he reached Laurel Bank, Mr. Bagshott,

having vented the full force of his rage upon the
bewildered Robert, had also got down to the root of the
matter. He had dragged from Robert the facts about the
elderly labourer, and he had dragged the elderly
labourer out of the local pub and extorted from him a
description of the scoundrel who had perpetrated the
outrage. The description could apply to none other than
Colonel Peabody. In this dastardly fashion had his
enemy tried to score off him and to avenge himself
because he had been worsted in argument. He set off at
once to challenge him and ran into him at the gate.
Robert and Dulcie watched and listened in fascinated
horror. . . . It was some time, of course, before either
of the two men could make out what the other was
talking about. Both talked together, both hurled insults,
both threatened legal proceedings. Then the onset on
either side slackened, and it was possible to hear
something of what was being said. Each was accusing the
other of deliberately ruining his garden, and each was
hotly denying the accusation. A faint note of bewilderment crept into the battle.

"I've got the man's word that it was you who ordered
the outrage."

"The description given to me couldn't apply to
anyone but you."

"That you should deliberately destroy the work of
years out of petty spite. . . . It's unthinkable, but you
shall pay for it. You shall pay for it!"

"My dear fellow, don't be absurd."

The "My dear fellow" somehow made it difficult to
continue the intensive stage of the argument. The
complexion of both had faded from purple to brick red.

"Perhaps there's been some mistake," said Mr.
Bagshott feebly. "Let's—let's talk it over."

They entered Mr. Bagshott's garden—that unadorned expanse of freshly dug soil which had so lately blossomed with roses and every variety of herbaceous plant.

The sight roused Mr. Bagshott's ire afresh.

"Vandalism," he muttered. "Hunnish vandalism! Gad! you shall pay for it, sir!"

But Colonel Peabody was picking up one of the catalogues that Robert had dropped in his agitation. He turned over the pages, frowning thoughtfully.

"I say!" he said. "You never get—what are they called—sweet peas this size really, do you?"

"Indeed I do," said Mr. Bagshott indignantly. "*Quite* that size. It's all a matter of culture."

Must say they'd brighten the place up," said Colonel Peabody thoughtfully.

"They do indeed," said Mr. Bagshott. "They do indeed." He in his turn had picked up the other catalogue that Robert had dropped. He pointed derisively to the picture of an onion on the front page. "Onions this size!" he said with a snort. "I ask you!"

"I've grown them quite that size," protested Colonel Peabody. "They need feeding, of course. Dried blood and the like. It's a science, of course, and you've never taken any interest in it."

"And tomatoes," said Mr. Bagshott, turning over a page. "I've never understood the fuss people make over them. They seem most uninteresting to me."

"Uninteresting?" echoed Colonel Peabody indignantly. "They're anything but uninteresting. Listen. This is how I grow mine."

Evidently there was to be a truce for the moment.

Robert and Dulcie heaved a sigh of relief and burst out laughing.

"It's all right," said Dulcie. "Quite definitely Uncle George is going to try onions and tomatoes."

"And I bet Colonel Peabody's going to have a shot at sweet peas," said Robert. "Do you know," he went on, "I've been trying to get to know you for weeks."

"I know you have," said Dulcie demurely. "Well, you've managed it at last."

Thereupon they began to talk. They found that they had quite a lot to talk about. . . . The minutes flew by. The two men continued to discuss the catalogues.

"Yes, yes," said Colonel Peabody. "Perhaps I've been shortsighted in the matter. A few flowers do brighten the place up. Properly tended of course. . . ."

"I see, I see," said Mr. Bagshott. "Their culture must be definitely interesting. Sowing for successive crops. And, now I come to think of it, the doctor did say that if I ate more vegetables, my rheumatism would be better."

Each admitted having given orders for a small part of his garden to be dug up. They admitted it reluctantly, shamefacedly.

"I—I did ask them to come round and dig up the few vegetables I had here," said Mr. Bagshott. "I hadn't realised, of course. . . . Cauliflowers now. Are they much trouble? They're one of the few vegetables I really enjoy."

"I—Well, I asked them to come round to take up the few old roses and plants I had," said Colonel Peabody. "I may have acted hastily. They were old plants, and the newer varieties are much more interesting, I realise that. . . . And, after all, one wants a little colour in life. But why on earth they should send someone to the wrong house and dig up the whole garden——"

Just then Dulcie, who was still standing with Robert at the gate, gave a scream.

"Goodness!" she said. "The gate's got the wrong name on. It's got 'Heather Bank'."

"*What!*" said Mr. Bagshott. He hurried down to the

gate to investigate. "Good Lord! Someone's altered the name. . . . Shouldn't wonder", to Colonel Peabody, "if they've put 'Laurel Bank' on your gate. A practical joke of course. . . . It explains the gardener's mistake."

"Shocking!" spluttered Colonel Peabody. "I—I— shall go to the police at once. I shall not rest till the rascal—whoever he is—is brought to justice."

"Well, well, well," said Mr. Bagshott soothingly. "Let's all go indoors and have a cup of tea first. Come along, old man," to Colonel Peabody. "I'm sure you're tired."

"Thanks, old fellow," said Colonel Peabody. "Very kind of you. Yes, by Jove, I could do with a cup of tea."

They turned towards the house, which Colonel Peabody had not entered since the quarrel.

You should try a few chrysanthemums, old man," said Mr. Bagshott. "Good varieties, of course."

"I certainly will," said Colonel Peabody. "I certainly will. . . . And you should try some asparagus. Quite easy to grow."

"I will, you may depend upon it," said Mr. Bagshott. "Those onions now . . . and cauliflowers. . . . Wonderful!" He looked over his shoulder at Robert and Dulcie. "Bring the young man in to have a cup of tea, Dulcie," he called. "I guess he needs it. . . ."

*   *   *

That evening Robert sat pretending to read a book. He was still in a state of bemused ecstasy after two hours spent in the company of Dulcie. Dulcie had proved even more adorable at close quarters than she had seemed in the distance. The two old men had renewed their friendship and had humbly received advice from each other on the growing of flowers and vegetables. They had discussed the mystery of the changing of the names on the gates without coming to any conclusion. They had notified the police and had sent Robert, armed with a screw-driver, to restore the names to their rightful places. Dulcie had accompanied him. They had taken a long time over it. When finally they parted, they felt, they said, as if they had known each other for years. . . .

Robert, holding his book upside down, was living again those rapturous moments in memory, when William entered the room. William carried his bow and arrow. He had evolved a new—and, he thought, original—idea for making his arrows particularly deadly to parachutists by fastening a bent pin on to the end of them. He had fastened them on with cotton taken from his mother's work-box, but they kept coming off.

"Bet I'll try glue nex' time," he said. "I bet glue'll fix 'em all right, don't you, Robert?"

Robert grunted.

He was thinking how charming was Dulcie's faintly tip-tilted nose. . . .

"If they don't stick on then." said William, "I'll try cotton again an' tie it on tighter. Which d'you think'd be best, Robert—glue or cotton?"

Robert grunted again.

He was thinking how lovely were Dulcie's deep blue eyes—like pools or—or delphiniums or something.

"Well, I think I'll try cotton again an' tie it tighter," said William, who was accustomed to grown-up grunts in answer to his questions. "Come to that, I could use glue *an*' cotton." He chuckled suddenly as at some gratifying memory. "I bet those names' get 'em muddled up all right. Bet when they see Laurel Bank where they thought Heather Bank was——"

Robert woke with a start from his reverie.

"*What!*" he demanded. "What on earth d'you mean?"

"Well," chuckled William, "I changed Laurel Bank an' Heather Bank round so's to get the parachutists all muddled."

Robert put down his book and stared at him.

"So it was you who played that fool trick," he began sternly, then suddenly reconsidered his attitude. After all, if William hadn't played that fool trick, he wouldn't have had the roseate memories that were now filling his mind, wouldn't have had that prospect of a walk with Dulcie to-morrow afternoon that filled his whole future with radiance. . . .

"What trick?" demanded William.

"Nothing," said Robert loftily. "I didn't hear what you said. Go away. I'm busy. . . ."

Chapter 10

Claude Finds a Companion

"They say there's not goin' to be any soon," said William. "They jus' aren't goin' to *make* 'em soon."

"Gosh!" said Ginger. "Fancy havin' to go without *sweets*!"

"I say," said William, "why shu'nt we start makin' sweets an' sell 'em to the sweetshops?"

"Why not eat 'em ourselves?" said Douglas simply.

"Oh, yes. Eat 'em ourselves, too. But I bet the sweetshops'll pay any amount for 'em now they can't get 'em ordin'ry. We can make enough to eat as many as we want ourselves an' get lots an' lots of money from the sweetshops as well."

The prospect was a roseate one. Too roseate, they felt, for reality. Henry voiced the obvious objection.

"You've gotter have special machinery for makin' sweets. They make 'em in factories."

"You can make 'em at home all right," said William. "They make 'em at home for Sales of Work an' things. They call 'em 'Home Made Sweets'. We'll call ours 'Home Made Sweets' an' we'll get lots an' lots of money for 'em an' have as many to eat as we want ourselves."

"How d'you make 'em?" said Ginger.

"Oh, you jus'—sort of mix things up together," said William vaguely. "Ethel once made some for a Sale of

Work, an' she jus—sort of mixed things up together."

"What sort of things?" demanded Douglas.

"Oh—I bet we can find out," said William with his usual optimism. "Sugar an' stuff."

"You can't get sugar," Douglas reminded him.

"I remember hearin' someone say", said Henry thoughtfully, "that you could make a sort of choc'late out of tinned milk an' cocoa. You jus' mix 'em."

"We'll jus' mix 'em, then," said William. "*Told* you it'd be quite easy."

"We've gotter make other sweets as well as chocolate," said Henry.

"I bet that's easy enough, too," said William. "All we've gotter do is to find out what to mix an'—an' jus' mix it."

"I was staying with an aunt once." said Ginger, "an' she was makin' Coconut Ice for a Sale of Work. She jus' mixed coconut an' sugar. I got into an awful row for eatin' it, too!" he ended simply.

"I jus' told you, you can't *get* sugar," Douglas reminded him.

"Well, there's other sweet things that'd do as well," said William. "Syrup an' honey an' stuff"—vaguely. "We'll have to 'speriment a bit, of course. . . . Tell you what. We'll all try 'n' get stuff from home to 'speriment with an' we'll do it here. Tinned stuff. Cocoa an' syrup an' coconut an' suchlike."

"Gosh!" said Ginger. "We'd get in an awful row takin' tinned stuff now. Well, they jus' wouldn't let us."

"No," agreed William. "We'll have to—sort of borrow it. We can pay it back when we're makin' a lot of money later on, same as we're goin' to. They'll be jolly grateful to us then. They'll be jolly glad we took it. I bet they'll thank us all right, then."

The other Outlaws tried to imagine grateful families

thanking them for purloining tinned food from their store cupboards in war time—and imagination balked at the attempt. Still, the prospect of experimenting was attractive, and William's picture of the boundless wealth that was to accrue to them as the result, more attractive still.

"I've heard of people makin' money out of a war," William was saying. "I couldn't think how to do it before. I tried wood but it didn't come off. I bet this is the way, all right. Stands to reason that the shops'll be jolly glad to buy our sweets when they can't get others an' they'll jolly well have to pay for 'em, too. Shouldn't be surprised if we ended up as rich as Lord Nuffield. I've always wanted to be as rich as Lord Nuffield."

Four future Lord Nuffields went home, to turn into four rather apprehensive small boys making furtive raids upon their mothers' store cupboards.

They met again at the old barn in the afternoon and displayed the result of their activities. William proudly exhibited a tin of cocoa and a small bottle of lemon curd.

"I bet lemon curd's all right," he said. "It's sweet. It'll do instead of sugar."

Ginger had brought a small bag of desiccated coconut and some tinned milk.

Henry had brought a tin of syrup and Douglas a tin of sardines.

"It's all I could find," said Douglas apologetically, "an' I thought it was better than nothin'."

"Yes, I bet it'll be all right," said William. "I don't see why you shouldn't have sardines in sweets. It'd be somethin' new, anyway. It'd be a good thing to have somethin' new. It'd sort of make the shops more int'rested in us. Sardine Toffee. It oughter be jolly good. Where's that bowl?"

William had thoughtfully abstracted a mixing bowl

from the kitchen while Emma's back was turned and had as well brought a large wooden mixing spoon. He set the bowl in the middle, brandished the spoon and said: "Now, what'll we do first?"

"Let's mix cocoa an' tinned milk an' make chocolate," suggested Ginger.

"No, let's try the coconut an' syrup," said Henry.

"I bet the Sardine Toffee'll be the best of all," said Douglas a little doubtfully. "Let's put a bit of syrup with 'em an' try it."

"Yes," said William with interest. "I bet it'll be all right. If it is, we can get a sort of patent for it. You get a *jolly* lot of money for patents. . . . Come on, let's try the choc'late first."

Ginger produced the bowl and William emptied the tinned milk and cocoa into it, then stirred it with the spoon. The others watched, breathless with eagerness.

"Doesn't look much like choc'late to me," said Ginger, inspecting the result. "Let's have a taste."

They tasted in turn, screwing up their faces into appraising grimaces.

"S" not *bad*," said Henry, "but it's not sweet enough. Let's put the syrup in."

They added the tin of syrup and tasted the result again.

"'S a bit *too* sweet now," said Ginger, "an' a bit too runny."

"Let's put the coconut in," suggested William. "That'll sort of soak it up."

They put in the coconut, stirred the whole mixture together, and tasted again.

"Tastes all right," said Ginger. "but it's still a bit too runny."

"Let's put the lemon curd in," suggested William. "The lemon curd's sort of stiff. It'll sort of stiffen it up."

The result was deemed fairly satisfactory. The only drawback was that it left the tin of sardines high and dry and nothing to mix with it.

"Look here," said William, "let's put the sardines in an' call the whole thing Sardine Toffee. The sardines'll give it a more *def'nite* taste than it's got now."

They emptied the tin of sardines into the mixture and beat it up till it was thoroughly incorporated in the whole.

"Now let's have a taste," said William.

He tried an experimental spoonful.

"Jolly good," he commented, blinking. "Sort of funny but—jolly good."

The others in turn each took an experimental spoonful. They too voted it "Sort of funny, but jolly good."

"What'll we do with it?" said Ginger.

"Well," said William, "it's jolly good Sardine Toffee, but it's no good keepin' this lot. We've found out how to make it, an' that was what we wanted to do. We may's well eat this lot."

The others agreed, crowding round for their turns with the spoon. The mixture slowly vanished. There was perhaps more than they had realised at first, but it was so delicious that it seemed a pity not to eat it all. Delicious it certainly was, and yet it left a curious after-taste—an after-taste that became gradually more and more curious till it completely drowned the original one. Douglas's countenance wore a greenish hue as he turned away from his last spoonful.

"I think I'll be goin' home," he said faintly.

The greenness of Douglas's face seemed to be reflected in the faces of the others. Even William's looked slightly pallid.

"Guess I'll be gettin' along now, too," muttered Henry.

"Gosh!" said William suddenly. "I've jus' remembered. It's Violet Elizabeth's birthday party. We're all s'posed to be there by four."

"Don't think I can go." said Douglas, his face growing a trifle greener at the words "birthday party", "I—I feel sort of peculiar. I bet it's that cold meat we had for lunch. Cold meat's enough to make anyone sick."

"Don't think I'll be able to come either," said Henry. "I feel a bit peculiar, too. I bet it was that sago puddin' we had for lunch. Always said it was sickenin' stuff."

"It'll be you an' me, then, Ginger," said William, turning his pallid countenance to Ginger's greenish one.

"Y-yes," agreed Ginger without enthusiasm.

A little later William, clean and tidy but still pallid, called for Ginger, and Ginger, clean and tidy but still greenish, set off with him for the party. They walked together down the road towards the Hall, slowly and in silence. A curious oppression lay over them. William made an effort to overcome the oppression and to conquer the strange qualms that kept disturbing his internal equilibrium.

"It'll be jolly nice to go to a birthday party, won't it?" he said. "Ices an' jellies an' suchlike."

Ginger's countenance took on a yet more decided shade of green. He stopped.

"I think I'd better go back home," he said in a far-away voice. "I—I—think——"

He turned unceremoniously and began hastily to retrace his steps.

William hesitated. His rash mention of "ices an' jellies an' suchlike" had intensified the qualms that already troubled him. He wondered whether to follow Ginger's example and return . . . but he was a boy who never liked to own himself beaten. Walking slowly, his face pale and set, he went on alone towards the Hall.

* * *

Mrs Dayford had come over to give a lecture at the Women's Institute on Child Psychology and had stayed the night at the Hall with Mrs. Bott. On hearing that Violet Elizabeth Bott's seventh birthday was to be celebrated the next day, she had hinted that she would like to be present, and, though Violet Elizabeth herself showed little appreciation of the honour thus done her, Mrs. Bott felt obliged to invite her to it.

Mrs. Dayford was a self-styled expert on Child Psychology and was always ready to give lectures and advice on the subject free of charge. She had evolved a new theory on child training and was anxious that it should have all the publicity possible. The theory was No Discipline but Suitable Mixing. The child should never be punished, but strong rough children should be mixed with quiet gentle ones. Thus, according to the theory, the gentle children become more manly and the rough ones more gentle.

Her son Claude, she considered to belong to the manly fearless type. In the opinion of less prejudiced judges he was an overfed, spiteful, undisciplined bully. Naturally Mrs. Dayford had applied her theories to his upbringing and had tried always to provide him with a quiet gentle companion. In his own district the supply of quiet gentle companions had long since run out. After the treatment they received at the manly Claude's hands, they seldom returned, and indeed in the majority of cases the visits ended abruptly, long before the arranged date. So that at present Claude was without that gentle angelic companion so necessary to his development.

It was partly the difficulty of finding a companion for Claude from among the children near his own home that had made Mrs. Dayford anxious to attend Violet

Elizabeth's birthday party. Perhaps among the guests at the party she could find a quiet gentle boy whose parents would realise what benefit he would derive from Claude's company and who would agree to her taking him home with her. . . . She was starting almost immediately on a lecture tour in the North and she wanted to get things fixed up as soon as possible. She didn't want to leave darling Claude without a companion on whom to impress his manliness.

Mrs. Bott had long since regretted her invitation, Mrs. Dayford had a way of throwing her weight about, and she took charge of the preparations for Violet Elizabeth's birthday party as if the whole thing had been her own idea. She was aghast at the amount of sweet cakes, pastries, jellies, blancmanges, and trifles provided by Mrs. Bott.

"In *war* time!" she expostulated. "It's dreadful."

"But it's Vi'let Elizabeth's birthday," protested Mrs. Bott. "It's not as if it was every day."

"That's no excuse," said Mrs. Dayford sternly. "No excuse at all."

A little of Mrs. Dayford went a long way, and by this time she had worn Mrs. Bott down. As a rule Mrs. Bott could give as good as she got, but she was just recovering from flu, so that things in general and Mrs. Dayford in particular were too much for her. She was on the verge of tears.

"Well, reely," she said, "I don't know what to do. I——"

"I'll tell you what we'll do," said Mrs. Dayford, with the air of one rising magnificently to an Occasion. "We'll appeal to the children's honour and sense of patriotism. We'll leave all the food just as you've put it out, and we'll appeal to the children to eat as little as possible, so that the rest may be sent to any evacuees there may happen to be in the neighbourhood. It will be good practice in self-sacrifice and self-control."

Mrs. Bott agreed despondently. It evidently wasn't going to be her sort of party at all, but she didn't feel equal to putting up a fight.

"You'll set an example to your little guests, won't you, dear?" said Mrs. Dayford to Violet Elizabeth. "You'd like your little guests to show a spirit of self-sacrifice, wouldn't you?"

Violet Elizabeth smiled sweetly and preserved an enigmatic silence. She was a self-centred child, and she didn't care whether her little guests showed a spirit of self-sacrifice or not. She had watched the preparations for the tea and knew exactly what her own mode of procedure was going to be.

The speech by which Mrs. Dayford urged the little guests to show patriotism and self-sacrifice was lengthy and eloquent.

"Remember, dear children," she ended, "that we are at war. Remember that we must all display the spirit of patriotism and self-control. We must eat, of course, in order to live, but let us show a spirit of service and comradeship this afternoon by eating as little as possible—as *little* as *possible*, dear children—so that what is left may go to the strangers we have welcomed into our midst, the evacuees."

She sat down amidst an applause that marked, not so much approval of the sentiments she had expressed as relief that the speech was over and that the real business of the day might now begin. As one man the little guests fell upon the feast outspread before them. The thought that the residue was to go to the evacuees had whetted their appetites. Not one but had suffered at the hands of the evacuees (tough young guys from the East End of London whose methods of warfare were novel and

"LET US SHOW A SPIRIT OF SERVICE AND COMRADESHIP THIS AFTERNOON BY EATING AS LITTLE AS POSSIBLE—AS *LITTLE* AS *POSSIBLE*, DEAR CHILDREN," SAID MRS. DAYFORD.

unpleasant) and the thought that their tormentors might profit from their abstinence urged them on to yet greater feats of gastronomy.

Mrs. Dayford watched them sadly. Jellies, trifles, blancmange, biscuits, cakes, disappeared as if at the wave of a magician's wand. None of these children appeared to be responding to her appeal—except one, and Mrs. Dayford's eye dwelt upon him with interest and approval. He was a boy of about eleven, who sat quietly by himself, not speaking to anyone around him. He had an intent pale face and a deeply earnest expression. She had noticed his eyes fixed upon her with an expression that could only be described as soulful

while she was speaking, and he at least seemed to have
been impressed by what she said. . . . He sat now with
his eyes turned resolutely away from the dainties before
him as if determined to avoid temptation. He ate, she
noticed, only a small piece of bread and butter. . . .

She approached her hostess.

"Who is that boy over there?" she said.

Mrs. Bott followed her gaze. "Er—William Brown,"
she said after a moment, for just at first she hadn't
recognised him.

"Where does he live?" asked Mrs. Dayford.

Mrs. Bott told her where William lived.

*   *   *

William walked slowly home. The fresh air had made
him feel a little better. He had just managed to hold on
through the party, though there had been a moment, on
first seeing the jellies and trifles spread out before him
and around him, when he had feared that the worst was
going to happen. . . . He couldn't say that he had
actually enjoyed the party, but he was not sorry that he
had gone to it. He never liked to feel that he had missed
anything. . . .

In ordinary circumstances Mrs. Brown would have
noticed that her younger son's countenance lacked its
usual hue of health, but Mrs. Brown was worried. Her
favourite sister was ill, and she would have liked to go
down for a few days and help nurse her, but she could not
leave William. Emma had declared most emphatically
that if she were "left with that there young limb" she
would pack her things and decamp without notice.

Moreover, everything in the house seemed to be
going wrong at the same time. The electric light had
fused, the outlet pipe in the bathroom was blocked, the
kitchen fire was smoking, and now Emma reported the

disappearance of a tin of cocoa and a jar of lemon curd from the store cupboard since morning.

"An', if you ask me, it's that there young limb, mum," she had added darkly. "I seed 'im snoopin' about there after lunch."

So that, when William reached home, Mrs. Brown was in no mood to give sympathetic consideration to the finer shades of his complexion.

"William," she began sternly, "if you've been to the store cupboard again, I shall tell your father."

William assumed a blank expression.

"The what, Mother?" he asked.

"The store cupboard," said Mrs. Brown shortly. "You heard what I said."

"When?" said William, playing for time.

"It doesn't matter when," said Mrs. Brown. "Have you been to the store cupboard to-day or have you not? Because if you've taken that cocoa and lemon curd——"

At the words "cocoa and lemon curd" a yellowish shade invaded William's pallor, but he clung doggedly to his blank expression and said:

"What store cupboard, Mother?"

"*William!*" said Mrs. Brown in exasperation. "There's only one store cupboard and——"

It was at this point that Mrs. Dayford was announced. She found the clean, pale, earnest-looking boy who had attracted her so at the party as clean and pale and earnest-looking as ever, not shouting or romping about as a boy of Claude's type would have been doing, but engaged in serious converse with his mother. It was *just* the boy she wanted for Claude. How good Claude's manliness would be for him! How good his gentleness and earnestness would be for Claude!

"Run away for the present, William," said Mrs. Brown shortly.

Mrs. Dayford watched him with approval as he went—still pale and earnest-looking—from the room.

Mrs. Brown had, of course, met Mrs. Dayford at the Women's Institute and had listened without much interest to her exposition of her System. She listened— still without much interest—to Mrs. Dayford's plan of taking back a quiet gentle boy to be Claude's companion. It was some time before she realised that she was proposing to take back William in this capacity. When she did realise it she couldn't believe it.

"You don't mean *William!*"she gasped.

But evidently Mrs. Dayford did mean William. She had met William at Violet Elizabeth's birthday party and thought him just the sort of boy she wanted as Claude's companion.

"He's so much *quieter* and *gentler* than Claude," she said.

Mrs. Brown tried to imagine Claude, and her imagination boggled at the task. She had decided by now that the whole thing was a dream, but in the dream Mrs. Dayford was waiting for her decision, so in the dream she must, of course, make it.

She considered the subject. William's absence from home for a short time (and it would be, she suspected, a very short time) would be convenient at this particular juncture. It would give her time, anyway, to run down and see her sister. But there was William himself to be considered. William generally had strong objections to leaving his home and his friends.

She called him in and put the proposition to him. Normally William would have indignantly repudiated the suggestion of going to stay with Mrs. Dayford, whom he disliked intensely. But just now it offered a welcome escape from an unwelcome interview with his father which he saw looming ahead of him. The visit would, of course, cause him to postpone the plans he had made for sweet-making on a large scale, but just at the minute he thought it as well that those plans should be postponed. The memory of Sardine Toffee—magnificent invention though it undoubtedly was—still caused those curious and unpleasant disturbances in the region of his stomach.

"Yes, Mother," he said meekly. "I'd like to go very much, thank you."

Mrs. Dayford's eyes rested on him with ever-increasing approval. Mrs. Brown, who had confidently expected a blunt refusal, stared at him in amazement.

"W-well," she said uncertainly, "it's very kind of you. . . . I shall have to ask his father, of course."

"I can let you have references," said Mrs. Dayford. "You could ring them up now, couldn't you? I'd like to take the little man back with me to-night."

"I'd like to go, please, Mother," said the little man

"Well——" said Mrs. Brown again helplessly and went to telephone her husband.

Mr. Brown was at first frankly incredulous, but quite willing that William should go.

"He'll be back on the next train, of course," he said, "but it'll give us a few hours' peace."

The references were satisfactory. William was unusually helpful in packing his things and within half an hour was setting off with his hostess-to-be for the station. Mrs Brown stood on the doorstep, watching his retreating back view, still feeling that it was all a dream. . . .

.   *   *   *

The chief members of Mrs. Dayford's household were Uncle Eustace, a timid studious little man who had long ago chosen the path of least resistance and allowed himself to be completely managed by his strong-willed niece, a housekeeper, and a gardener. The touch of nature that made the whole household kin was a hearty dislike for Master Claude—a dislike to which none of them dared give expression. Uncle Eustace dared not even box his ears, no matter what the provocation—and often the provocation was immense. The housekeeper and gardener had to endure the manliness of Claude without retaliation or get another place, and Mrs. Dayford paid her employees well. She had found that it was necessary. All of them bitterly resented Claude's treatment of the quiet gentle companions whom his mother obtained for him, but—there was nothing to be done about it. Uncle Eustace groaned when he heard that yet another angelic child was coming to be sacrificed on the altar of Claude's manliness. He groaned still more deeply when he learnt that his niece would be away during the angelic child's visit. He knew what it would mean. It would mean that a weeping small boy would continually be coming to him with complaints, and interference on his behalf was strictly forbidden. It prevented, his niece explained, the full free working of her System. As the hour drew nearer for the arrival of his niece and the new companion, he became more and more depressed.

They did not arrive till after Claude was in bed, and the new boy was despatched to bed immediately. Uncle Eustace thought, with interest, that, though pale, he looked a little more sturdy than the boys chosen as Claude's companions usually looked.

"I shall have to go to catch my train before the boys are up," his niece said to him. "You'll keep an eye on them—won't you?—but on no account interfere, of course. William's such a timid little soul. He needs some of Claude's manliness, and Claude would do well to acquire some of this dear child's gentle, earnest nature."

The next morning Uncle Eustace introduced the two boys to each other and sent them off to play. He inspected the new boy with renewed interest. He looked less pale this morning, and even sturdier than he had looked last night.

"Come on," said Claude. "Let's go to the pond."

William accompanied him in silence. He was taking stock of Master Claude and so far didn't think much of him. The pond was at the far end of the garden, and a plank stretched from the edge to an island in the middle. What water there was was fairly shallow. Most of it was mud.

"Let's go over the plank to the island," suggested Claude.

"A'right," agreed William.

"You go first," said Claude, "an' I'll hold the plank steady for you."

"A'right," said William.

He was not entirely without doubts, but he had decided to give Claude the benefit of them for the present. He took about a dozen steps along the plank, then Claude twisted it, with the skill of one much practised in that particular sleight of hand, and William was precipitated into the mud. He managed to land on his feet, but the mud reached up to his knees. Slowly he waded back to the bank. Slowly he approached Claude, who was dancing with glee and uttering shouts of jeering triumph. He feared no retaliation. None of his former companions had even attempted it.

At this point Uncle Eustace happened to glance out of his study window. The new boy and Claude were together at the edge of the pond. The new boy was more or less coated with mud, as new boys generally were after a little frolic with Claude down by the pond. Only one thing made the spectacle different from the many similar ones Uncle Eustace had witnessed before. The new boy wasn't crying. . . . This interested Uncle Eustace, and he stayed to see what would happen next. What happened next interested him still more. For the new boy had taken Claude by the collar, hauled him wriggling to the edge of the pond, and pushed him down in the mud on his face. Claude scrambled to his feet and came, bawling and yelling, back to the house. . . .

Uncle Eustace moved hastily away from the window, rubbing his hands and smiling a little smile of satisfaction.

Upstairs the housekeeper received the bawling Claude and dried and changed him with barely concealed delight.

Outside in the garden William waited apprehensively. He was aware that he had been invited here in order to be a "companion" to Claude, and he was aware that companions who push their little hosts into the mud do not thereby endear themselves to their little hosts' parents and guardians. He had had provocation, but experience had taught him that parents and guardians do not recognise provocation as an excuse for the maltreatment of their dear ones.

Suddenly he saw Claude coming down to him from the house, clean and changed and tidy. To his relief Claude's face wore a friendly smile. Evidently the little incident was to be regarded as merely an exchange of civilities, from which normal relations could now take their start. He had pushed William into the mud, been pushed in himself by William, and so they were quits. Claude was not quite such a sportsman as this, but he was feeling fairly cheerful. He had relieved his feelings by kicking the housekeeper on the shins, by hiding Uncle Eustace's *Times*, which he had left on the hall table, behind the umbrella stand, and calling at the greenhouse, where he had mixed all the gardener's seeds together and dropped a bag of fertiliser into the rain tub. There remained his little companion to be dealt with, and Claude had no doubts of his ability to do that. He had had plenty of practice in dealing with little companions. . . . He didn't quite know what had happened at the edge of the pond. He must have lost his balance somehow. The little companion must now pay for that with interest.

He approached William with a grin, then suddenly put out his hand to tweak William's nose. He received a blow on his own that sent him staggering backwards. The unexpected pain lent temporary fury to his attack. He flung himself on William, bellowing with rage. He was bigger than William but a less skilled fighter. He received another blow on the nose, one in the eye, and a specially neat one on the chin. . . . The fight was not without an audience. Uncle Eustace was watching from behind the study curtain, quite unaware that he was waving his arms about as if himself taking part in the fight on William's side. The housekeeper was watching from an upstairs window. She had had to limp to get there—for Claude's shoes were heavy and he had kicked hard—but her face wore a smile of ecstasy as she watched. The gardener stood at the door of the greenhouse. He had found his mixed seeds and ruined fertiliser, and knew it to be the work of Master Claude. . . . Less discreet than the other two, he yelled: "Go to it, lad. . . . Give 'un one on his buzzer."

The end of the fight was not in doubt for long. A "corker" from William on the side of Claude's face sent him on to the ground. He got up to run, met William's fist once more, and went down again like a ninepin. Finally he picked himself up and escaped homewards, with blood streaming from his nose, bawling more

UNCLE EUSTACE WAS WATCHING FROM BEHIND THE STUDY
CURTAIN.

loudly than ever. The audience at once vanished. No one
was to be seen at Uncle Eustace's window, at the
housekeeper's, or at the greenhouse door.

It was, of course, an unprecedented situation. Always
before it had been the companion who had run yelling to
the house, denouncing Claude and demanding justice,
to be met with the bland evasive policy of non-
interference so firmly laid down by Claude's mother.

Claude went first to the housekeeper blubbering
loudly and demanding William's punishment. She

CLAUDE WAS BIGGER THAN WILLIAM BUT A LESS SKILLED
FIGHTER.

bathed his bleeding nose and black eye but seemed not
to hear when he complained of William, merely mur-
muring something quite irrelevant about the bruises on
her own shins.

Uncle Eustace was no better. He was absent-minded
and quite deaf to Claude's complaints, merely asking
him if he had seen his *Times* anywhere.

Meanwhile William remained in the garden, more
apprehensive than ever. His pushing Claude into the
mud might have been overlooked as "horse play", but
not the bashing of his nose and blacking of his eye. No,
retribution would now fall on him. He would be sent

home in disgrace, as his father had predicted he would be. And William did not want to be sent home. It was one of the finest gardens he had ever played in. The pond held innumerable possibilities. He didn't like Claude but he liked Uncle Eustace, the housekeeper, and the gardener. All these people now, of course, would be his mortal enemies. He wondered whether to run away. But it was too late. Already Uncle Eustace was coming across the lawn to him. He was "for it". . . . But Uncle Eustace seemed to know nothing of the fight. He ignored all signs of it—even Claude's yells that still rang out over the garden from the house. He talked vaguely of other things and led William to the peach house.

"Take one, my boy," he said. "Take two, take three, take four. . . ."

And trotted back to his study, smiling happily to himself.

Soon the gardener approached the door of the peach house. *Now* he was in for it, thought William. He knew gardeners. This one would never believe that Uncle Eustace had introduced him to the peach house, and in any case he had already taken five peaches, when Uncle Eustace had only said "Take four". But, to his amazement, the gardener took a couple of ripe plums from the pocket of his green baize apron, handed them to him with a wink and a grin and went on his way. William's bewilderment increased. He ate the plums, had a few more peaches, then walked slowly and still apprehensively back to the house. He paused uncertainly in the hall. He was pretty grubby. He'd better go and wash. His mother had impressed on him to wash frequently. . . .

Slowly and cautiously he made his way towards the staircase. As he was passing the kitchen door, it opened suddenly, and the housekeeper came out, carrying a bowl of hot water with which she was about to bathe the wounds of the battered Claude. She looked at William, darted back into the kitchen and reappeared almost immediately with a large piece of chocolate cake, which she slipped into his hand with what, though not quite a wink, was not very far off.

"There you are—you bad boy!" she said and went on up the stairs, carrying the hot water.

William stood gazing after her, dazed and bewildered.

* * *

He met Claude at lunch-time. Claude's nose was swollen and his eye a rich purple, but he did not appear to bear malice. Claude, though a bully, was no fool. He realised that he was no match for William, and he was not going to provoke him to another fight. He realised, too, that neither Uncle Eustace nor the housekeeper intended to punish William or interfere in any way, so he had decided to bide his time. He would carefully store up in his memory every grudge against William, and when his mother returned he would insist that a letter of complaint should be sent to William's parents. Mrs. Dayford was a masterful woman, but Claude could manage her. . . . Meantime, he would pretend to be friendly with William, would even pretend to follow him.

And, as the days went on, he found that it was no bad thing to follow William. He could not, indeed, restrain a grudging admiration for a boy who could climb to the top of the big oak tree, vault the gate, and walk along the top of the high brick wall that surrounded the kitchen garden.

The games of pirates and Red Indians which William had taught him were hitherto unknown and gloriously exciting. Despite himself he played them zestfully.

enjoying them more than he had ever enjoyed anything in his life before. William was certainly a change from the namby-pambys to whom he was accustomed. At first he kept the score religiously, making a mental note of every push and scuffle, every insult, every opprobrious nickname, every careless cuff. It was good to feel that retribution was coming to this bully and hooligan whom his mother, by some outrageous mistake, had inflicted on him. Together the two boys roamed the countryside, climbed trees, played pirates and Red Indians and other games of William's invention, and Claude found it more and more difficult to keep the score accurately.

Mrs. Dayford arrived home at the end of the week. She was delighted when she saw the two boys. Claude looked much fitter, while the new boy was absolutely transformed. It was difficult to believe that he was the pale wistful-looking child whom she had first seen at Violet Elizabeth's birthday party. Claude's manliness had improved him almost beyond recognition, and there was no doubt at all that this boy's gentleness had improved her darling Claude. The whole thing, in fact, was a triumphant justification of her System. She would start a new book on it straight away. . . .

She looked into Uncle Eustace's study.

"Everything gone all right, Uncle Eustace?" she said.

"I—I think so, my dear," said Uncle Eustace, raising his head from his book. "Oh yes—I think so."

"Our little William seems a trifle less timid and nervous."

"Er—yes," agreed Uncle Eustace. "Yes, certainly."

"And I think that darling Claude has learnt something from William's seriousness."

"Er—exactly," agreed Uncle Eustace again. "Oh, yes. Exactly."

Claude entered the room. He had enjoyed having

William to play with, but he wasn't going to be robbed of the great moment he had promised himself. His black eye was still an interesting shade of violet, and the whole household would bear witness that it owed its origin to William.

"Mother," he said, "I want to speak to you about William——"

Uncle Eustace sighed. He had suspected that this was going to happen, but experience had taught him that it would be useless to "interfere."

"Yes, dear," said Mrs. Dayford. "Oh, by the way, William's going home to-morrow. His mother wants him to catch the early train."

Claude's mouth dropped.

"Going—*home*?" he gasped.

Getting his own back was one thing, but losing a boy who knew the games that William knew was another.

"Yes, dear. His mother's come back from nursing her sister and they want William to start school again at once. *Claude!*" in sudden horror. "Where *did* you get that black eye?"

Uncle Eustace held his breath.

Claude gulped.

"I—I tripped over something and fell. . . . Mother, *can't* William stay?"

*   *   *

The next morning Mr. Brown received a letter that made him suspect for a moment that he was the victim of a practical joke. He read it through several times and, though its contents remained incredible, it was evidently genuine enough. For it spoke of the ennobling effect of William's "gentleness" and "quietness" and "seriousness" on the writer's own rougher and more noisy son. It assured Mr. and Mrs. Brown that they would find their little son less timid and nervous, that there was now some colour in his "pale little face" and, if they found him a little less serious-minded than before, there was perhaps no great harm in that.

Helplessly Mr. Brown handed the letter to his wife.

"When does William arrive?" he said.

"Half past eleven," said Mrs. Brown.

"Let me warn you", said Mr. Brown solemnly, "that we must look for a new William—a William mysteriously ennobled and transformed."

It is, perhaps, unnecessary to add that they looked in vain.

THE END